CW00920762

.L.

Watercolor, 1934

THE ILLUMINATED BURROW

"He's in a bad way," the nurse added. "His sores are leaking like a tap, and I've suspected for days something's not right with his lungs."

Indeed, a minute later he erupted into a long dry cough that rattled from the depths of his throat, as if he were suffocating or choking on a drink. The coughing, wheezing and spitting next door seemed like it would go on forever. I could hear his breathlessness, each inhalation more urgent and less certain, eventually followed by a moment's relief during which he asked for a drink of water.

The rest of the evening was filled with a variety of noises, which culminated in terrible bouts of coughing, until, exhausted, I fell asleep and didn't wake up till dawn, when my eyes opened suddenly as if a secret alarm had clicked in my subconscious, alerting me that this was the day of my operation. What a gloomy, dreary light I woke up to that morning! My heart was pounding, I was starving, tired and wretched, and that bleak dawn seemed to me the saddest and most bitter of my entire life. The operation was scheduled for ten a.m., and I had woken up at five, before the clinic was even open . . .

I will spare you the details of the operation, because I want to tell you about something else right now.

A few hours after I had been brought back from the operating theatre, I was lying on my bed, nearly unconscious. The only thing I remember was that nothing hurt and I was floating in an indescribable drowsiness that hollowed out my chest and made it impossible to grip onto any kind of solid, stable reality. At last, I was fully alert. All my muted pain flooded me again,

each ache awaking in turn, every one of them remembering its acuteness, vice-like pressure over here, sharp intermittent pangs over there, and my legs, which had been immobile for so long, were fizzing with a thousand itches that spread out under the skin as if an army of sewing machines were at once diligently at work to slice apart my flesh. But worst of all was the thirst scorching my throat. My mouth, my throat, my whole body seemed filled with an aridity, tasteless as dry, tepid ash.

In vain did I beg for water. I wasn't allowed to drink for six hours, and even then I was only allowed a spoonful of liquid. I was too weak to insist, to keep begging the nurse, and besides, I knew the water would only make me sick after the chloroform and prolong my agony. I resolved to wait, but a few minutes later I was again asking for a drink. No matter what logical rationales my mind came up with, they were promptly vanquished by the torpid, exhausting, burning thirst. Every sentence and reassuring thought that passed through my brain were consumed by a heat that turned them into dry husks, amplifying my agony with their haze of logic, a delirious whirl of rational, medical arguments gradually sinking into the slowly sifting ash of my all-consuming thirst.

On the table in front of me was the carafe of water, illuminated by a sunbeam that had sneaked in through the curtainless window. If I just stretched my arm a little I could touch it. But I was being guarded by a nurse who was sitting on the bed and reading the paper — the onset of a dull, sullen afternoon. An unbearable, oppressive atmosphere reigned in that unfurnished room, promising empty, tedious hours where nothing would

happen and there would be nothing to look forward to.

All of a sudden, we heard whispers and that familiar cough in the next room. I remembered the patient on the other side and asked the nurse how he was doing. Not well at all, the priest was with him at the moment to take his confession. Everything now made sense, as the whispers became more distinct and I recognised the priest's voice, urging the patient to submit to this final sacred rite while he stubbornly refused and protested when the cough allowed it:

"Please . . . leave me alone . . . I have my own beliefs . . ."

And as the priest's entreaties grew more pressing, the patient continued:

"Please leave me alone . . . I see no need to confess . . ."

I can hear those words ringing through my mind even today, in the same grave, dignified, lucid way he pronounced them:

"I see no need . . ."

His family made vain attempts to persuade him, but the patient flatly refused. Ultimately the priest had no choice but to leave. As it was, the patient had been seized by a dreadful cough and was now wheezing and spitting almost without pause.

"He's going to spit out the last piece of his lungs," the nurse remarked, her eyes still fixed on the newspaper. And in the same tone of voice: "Marlene Dietrich is coming to Paris . . . I'm dying to see her . . ."

My head was pounding terribly from thirst, from weakness, and possibly from the fever starting to burn me up. Everything I could hear, everything that was happening around me, was immersed in intense dizziness and confusion: I grasped every word that came out of the nurse's mouth, I understood perfectly everything happening around me, but it all seemed disconnected and implausible, each word discrete from the next, each event unrelated to one another, like a heap of rocks in a sack. The essential connections between them, the thread linking them together into meaning, and me to their reality, kept eluding me. It was as if I weren't even witnessing what was happening around me, as if fragments of reality were falling into the room and then evaporating, as if someone had carefully placed in that empty room on that afternoon a bed, a patient, a nurse, a few chairs, a connecting door, a priest, a dying man, and now a gigantic hand was pulling the strings of these marionettes who played their roles on this stage . . . "confess . . . no need . . . Marlene . . . water . . ."

My head was buzzing like a beehive. I sunk deeper into confusion and chaos for awhile, keeping my eyes riveted on a particular spot on the gramophone. It was quiet again on the other side of the door, the patient momentarily resting, but from the agitated whispers of his visitors and the frantic footsteps rushing out of the room to fetch a nurse, I could tell the situation was grave. In that instant, I felt something unusual happening to my body under the covers. The spot where I had been operated on was no longer painful but instead seemed warm and damp, and I felt something trickling down my leg.

When I informed the nurse of this, she lifted the covers and carefully examined the bandages.

"I'll call the matron," she announced after a long silence.

"What's happening?" I asked in alarm.

And when she didn't answer, I persisted.

"A small haemorrhage," she answered, with a slight pause. "Blood has seeped through the bandages and I think I should put a rubber mat underneath to keep the sheets from getting soiled. Please don't move, I'll be right back . . ."

And then she rushed out, leaving me alone with my body exposed on the bed.

All my attention was now focused again on the commotion next door, as I could hear the voice of the matron on the other side, which meant my nurse wouldn't be able to find her and I would be forced to lie in that uncomfortable position a while longer.

I suddenly remembered the carafe on the table. I was alone.

I knew taking a drink would worsen my condition, that I would be sick and suffer in myriad ways. But the thirst was agonising . . . I stretched my arm as far as I could, pushed myself a little further and cried out in pain as I disturbed my bandages, and then, triumphing over my agony, finally grabbed the carafe.

At that moment, the patient next door began to cough again. It was as if he'd been silently waiting for the moment I touched the carafe of water before launching into a fit.

I grabbed the carafe and greedily brought it to my lips.

I think sometimes life condenses around trivial events and becomes in that instant a thousand times weightier and more intense than usual, like stardust floating through space whose matter, we are told, is a thousand times denser than that of our planet. And I think I experienced that same condensation of life, unlike anything I had felt before, apart from on two or three occasions, when the water touched my lips. Some things are so fundamentally simple they cannot be put into words, and the first drop of water touching my lips was exactly like that. I try to find a word to describe the sensation and I can think of only one: delirious. That was it: a kind of delirium, scrambling my brains, making me burst into hoots of laughter or tears, making me grin like a madman! I felt like kissing the water rather than drinking it. I actually remember trying to "kiss" the water by pursing my lips and sloshing the liquid around my mouth. If I'd had a loaded gun in my hand and someone would have tried to take the water away from me, I have no doubt I would've pulled the trigger without hesitation, with as much relish, voluptuousness, and determination as I had when draining half the carafe of water.

When I placed the carafe back on the table, I felt light-headed for a few seconds, as if drunk (a cliché echoed, muffled, through my mind — "You're drunk on water!") or dropped out of a whirlwind that had spun me around, vertiginous to the point of fainting. How many years had passed since I drank the water?

It was as if a long, long time had slipped away, as if a new life had taken root inside me, as if by satisfying that thirst I had shed my parched, shrivelled body, that drained body which was now only a fading memory. It took me almost a minute to regain my senses. Then I floated back to the surface of reality, swimming towards greater and greater clarity, slipping back into my ordinary ways. When I was at last restored to full consciousness, I became aware of a deep silence. No noise reached me from beyond the door, something had surely just happened there, because the coughing fit that had started when I took the first sip of water had stopped, and so had the visitors' whispers, their footsteps, even their breathing, or so it seemed. It was a shocked silence. But it only lasted for a moment, and then a woman burst into tears, and then another, and soon I could hear a nurse asking them to step outside. Yet they protested, still weeping — "I want to see him, let me see him" — and their weeping grew more and more desperate, uncontrollable.

I understood what had happened — clearly, the patient had just passed.

It was an ordinary, insignificant afternoon, drifting by listlessly and monotonously. Nothing had changed in my room, the sunbeam had travelled from table to wall, the carafe of water was still in its place, and yet in that brief interval in which a ray of light travelled a few centimetres and I performed the simple act of satisfying my thirst, in that same moment a man experienced the most grave and momentous event of his existence: death. For a while I was disoriented, unable to process the significance of what had just happened, but as I struggled to engage with the full meaning of the experience, in time I realised I was too tethered to that banal, ordinary afternoon to be able to grasp the gravity of the moment of death. And yet, it seemed this was not an event I could dismiss lightly with a sceptical remark or a shrug of the shoulders.

Where does the significance of a moment lie? How can we recognise its profundity and resolute irreversibility? What makes the instant when a man dies different from all the others filled with ordinary, simple things? Every minute the momentous and the banal happen simultaneously while everything around you remains unchanged, just like the afternoon light and my body, which hides its living warmth inside a sack of skin. And when I close my eyes, they fill with the same darkness and I'm invaded by the usual visions: serious, simple, hallucinatory, extraordinary or hilarious, but all of them, without exception, completely unrelated to the death of any man. And this happens every second . . . every second . . . Appalling!

I often think of my own death and strain to imagine its every detail, to paint a precise picture of how it will happen, and I can easily construct various images or predict different pains or ways I might slip out of consciousness. Here I am, with my mouth agape, unable to close it again or draw another breath, as if the air has stopped at the opening of my mouth, powerless to push through (I imagine this as air dropping to the bottom of a sack, unable to go any further). And another vision, a medley of colours, lights and sounds becoming less and less distinct as I fall through them until I reach complete darkness, except that it's something sharper and denser than darkness or sensory deprivation, nothing easily put into words, but something quite definite, opaque and irremediable, especially irremediable, which I'm no longer a part of but am still, most radically, most essentially, a part of, all the way to the very depths of the darkness (which, in comparison to that state of unbeing, is still teeming with light) and then I fall out of life, just as I do when I inhale chloroform on the operating table.

Well, whatever my "own way" might be, whatever my pains or the scenario for my loss of consciousness, everything else in the world will remain fixed in its own familiar shape, and maybe in that same instant a man will stop in the street, take out a box of matches and light a cigarette. This is why I don't understand anything that happens around me and why I continue to "fall" through life, to fall between events and scenes, between minutes and people, between colours and music, more and more vertiginously, second by second, deeper and deeper, senselessly, like through a pit engraved with deeds and faces, and my "fall," which is nothing more than another body on its way towards the void, might also be called — inexplicably, bizarrely — "my life" ...

To put more flesh on this story and to explain even more clearly the strange diversity of everyday events, I would like to add that during the same evening I was made aware, somewhat grotesquely, of the import of my neighbour's death and the different reactions to this tragedy in the sanatorium.

Later that afternoon, almost evening, a good friend of mine came to see how I was doing. We were talking quietly when we heard a tumult from the other side of the door, the loud voices of porters and nurses, orders being given and furniture rearranged.

"Who's staying in that room?" my friend asked.

"No-one at the moment," I answered. "You might

remember a jaundiced fellow who dined with us for a couple days, he arrived with his mother and two stout, ruddy-cheeked sisters, he occupied the room until this afternoon, when he died. I think they must be cleaning up after him now and packing his things so they can send him off tomorrow morning."

For a few moments we were silent, listening to the commotion next door, then my friend started chuckling to himself.

"Why are you laughing?" I asked.

"I understand, now I understand," he answered. "I was puzzled by the supervisor's generosity . . ."

And then he explained that just as everyone was gathering for dinner, he passed the "office" on his way to my room and happened to overhear a conversation between a waiter and the director's wife, whom we used to call "the supervisor" as she was in charge of everything to do with the kitchen and the patients' meals.

"You know them," the supervisor was telling the waiter. "It's the woman in black and the two girls with ruddy cheeks."

"I know them," answered the waiter, "they usually sit at a table by the window."

"Please, Louis, take special care of them, give them generous portions of asparagus, some nice thick stems . . ."

After my friend finished reporting this brief conversation, he asked:

"You see? The supervisor wanted to console the family so she did the only thing she could, she made sure they were given a good portion of nice thick asparagus . . ."

And, after a pause:

"At the end of the day, there are conventional ways to think about the dead, to pay them respect. But when dealing with their grieving families, we do the best we can ... this could be the topic of a Pascalian meditation ... some of us comfort them with flowers, others with asparagus ..."

If, as I glide through life, the meaning and significance of each moment elude me, this might be because I elude them too, escaping into a closed world, a world inside me, secret and private. I suspect there might be slight difference between the exterior world and the realm of the imagination. While awake I have often seen such strange things that could only exist in dreams, and other times I have dreamt or imagined events and struggled to discern in what world, or reality, they took place.

To experience something or to dream it is, in my opinion, one and the same, and daily life is as hallucinatory and uncanny as a dream. Any attempt to precisely determine in which of those worlds I am writing these lines would end in failure. When I'm asleep, I dream enchanting poems, impeccably phrased and full of original images, which I recite as confidently as I now write this, and I confess that many images have floated into my mind during sleep, and when I awoke an echo of them persisted, clear and insistent, so the only thing I had to do was to grab a piece of paper and transcribe them. I also like to imagine that in the world of sleep there is at least a slim volume of verse bearing my signature, which the slumbering can read in their nightmares ...

I gaze around me in profound and utter astonishment, and

the shock is exactly the same whether I have my eyes open or shut.

A certain story has been playing out in my dreams for several years, and in recounting it here I cannot properly tell to which half of my life it belongs, because it is as coherent, or incoherent, in the light of day I submerge myself in as I pen it as it was in the bright sunlight of the "dream world" where these bizarre and melancholy events were staged. More melancholy than bizarre, I should say, and unintelligible rather than hallucinatory, just as everything else that happens in my life.

In that place at the edge of town I have been visiting every night in my dreams for so many years, I rest against a decrepit wall by the side of a dusty road full of potholes. A tall acacia tree spreads its canopy above, providing merciful shade in the unbearable summer heat. I lie in the grass under the shelter of a few enormous stones, the ruins of the wall behind me, and read my newspaper in peace. I feel good, just a little hot. On his way to the slums teeming with children, the ice cream vendor stops his cart in the shade of the acacia tree and looks for me by the rocks — he knows me well. He's a short young man of indeterminate age who wears an expression of perfect indifference. In short, with men like him the bloom of adolescence is abruptly replaced by the deep furrows of maturity while the skin still retains its smoothness. It's impossible to guess the age of such people, as their cheeks vaguely indicate an indefinite maturity for decades. Maybe the ice cream vendor is a very young man who has replaced one of his front teeth with sparkling gold in order to appear older, or maybe the gold tooth is a status symbol, in the same way that some wear a pin in their buttonhole to make a statement, and what it announces to the world is that he's the proud owner of an ice cream cart and shouldn't be confused with some crummy street hawker since he's managed to raise enough money to buy himself a shiny gold tooth. Or maybe he just needed a false tooth.

These are the thoughts running through my mind as I talk to him and his lips part as he speaks to reveal that flash of gold metal. But as I write this, I remember that when we were at college we used to buy ice cream in the summer and halva in the winter from a boy just like this one, whose gold tooth dazzled me as we shivered together in the quad during breaks . . .

Maybe the ice cream vendor from college is the very same one I meet on the deserted, dusty road of my dream, but then how can he "live" and sell ice cream in a dream as well as in the real world? Surely they must be two entirely different people. And still, they look so similar, amazingly so . . . I believe they are the same person . . . I don't believe anything anymore . . . I'm getting confused . . . Whenever I try to delineate the territory of the dream world from reality, everything becomes muddled and I give up. Anyway, that's not what I wanted to tell you about, I wanted to tell you about certain events that took place on that deserted road where normally nothing happens — certain surprising, extraordinary events.

For the past few years, the police station in our town has kenneled dogs to train them to catch criminals. The local newspaper ran a long article last year about this canine unit featuring a series of photographs, each one more evocative and impressive than the next. Some showed the dogs effortlessly climbing up fences, some showed them, ears pricked, sniffing a footprint while other dogs were jumping on the back of a policeman disguised as a robber, with his head covered by a blanket to protect his flesh from being shredded by the ferocious fangs of those perfectly trained beasts. I often saw the dogs on the street leashed to policemen on a mission, and they were outfitted in special uniforms to distinguish them from ordinary dogs. Truly — these dogs wore caps adorned with police insignia and special monogrammed jackets, S.P., Secret Police, beautiful jackets tailored from splendid, sky-blue cloth and embroidered with gold. This alone seemed bizarre to me.

In the newspaper photographs the dogs were not in uniform, and the point of these outfits was beyond me, since they would've only encumbered the dogs, slowed them down, and been ruined by the second or third time they clambered over a fence.

I have no way of finding out if this assumption is correct, but I can honestly say the dogs did indeed wear uniforms. They must have been in uniform when I saw them, only that . . . But I'll tell you what happened . . .

Well, these dogs, locked in the kennels where they were fed, communicated with one another through short barks, gently pawing the wooden cages, and discreetly tapping the walls — a kind of secret code that nobody else understood, for they were, after all, specially trained police dogs. Every day they were released from the kennels at various times to be groomed and have a chance to stretch their stiff limbs. But then, over a period of a few months, the policemen noticed something unusual happening to the dogs. At the time, no-one knew of their secret language, or that barking, pawing and tapping was how they communicated from cage to cage. When in the yard together, instead of frolicking, jumping and running around merrily, they would gather in groups of two or three, snout to snout, as if involved in secret discussions consisting of low whines and light touches which the policemen thought of no importance, something they would come to regret a few weeks later.

Because one day a revolution erupted. It happened just after feeding time, after the dogs had feasted heartily on their rations and drank their fill, when a sharp, authoritative bark summoned two dogs to guard the gate of the yard where they'd been fed. A second later, the rest of the dogs surrounded the guards who were clearing up the remainders of the food, and barking loudly and jumping on them from every direction, they forced the men to retreat into the kennels and bolted the doors from outside, caging the humans in the same way as they'd been caged.

Drowned out by the thunderous barking, the guards' cry for help was no use, and any attempt to escape futile. Two fierce hounds guarded the cages and no-one would defy their threatening fangs, and, in fact, the poor men were too befuddled by what was happening to even dare to protest.

When the gate of the courtyard opened, the dogs stormed

into the station either through the doors, which they had been trained to open, rising on their hind legs, or through the windows, which were open due to the summer heat.

And then the policemen inside suffered the same fate as the guards. Around eight of them were in the station, two commissioners, the chief of police and a secretary, and those thirty dogs used all their police training to ambush them before they had a chance to react and draw their guns. Yes, the dogs were well trained, and they used that excellent training designed to overpower bandits and rummage through their pockets to floor and disarm all the policemen. One of the dogs used his snout to open a drawer and retrieve some handcuffs which the others put on the policemen lying on the floor, many of them bitten and wounded, immobilised by other dogs who pinned them down with their paws.

When all the policemen's hands and feet had been shackled, the dogs sank their teeth into their uniforms and dragged them outside, then bundled them into the kennels. They were locked inside with the guards. When another policeman would come back from town later, they would keep an eye on him, let him come into the station, and then bring him down, throwing him in with the others. It was easy enough by then.

So the dogs ruled the roost in the police station by the time evening fell. They dispatched a team to bring provisions that same night, sending out dogs specially trained to break into locked houses, and this was how the butcher's shop got completely ransacked.

Over the coming days, no-one set foot in the police station, not even the poor butcher, who probably had his own reasons to avoid any meddling from the law. And besides, who cares what goes on in a provincial police station? A few days passed in this way, with the dogs lording it over the station and then sneaking out at night to break into various butcher's shops. Several such establishments as well as some well-stocked delicatessens were completely devastated. At the same time, with the police force out of action, petty crime and robberies spiralled out of control. With something clearly amiss in the town, a band of concerned citizens took it upon themselves to complain at the police station. Some of them went inside while the others waited for them in the yard.

And that spelled the end for the dogs.

When the delegation made its way into the corridor, the guard dogs raised the alarm, and the others, who had settled themselves in the offices, jumped to attention, but it wasn't enough to ward off the danger, for most of them were lounging on sofas or lay sprawled on the floor, stuffed with cold cuts, fat, lazy and lethargic. The people in the corridor could easily defend themselves. In addition, the ones who were waiting outside, hearing the screams and barks, rushed in to see what the fuss was about. Somehow they managed to escape without being torn to pieces. They had no idea what was going on, but suspecting something wasn't right, they called the fire brigade, who rushed inside and overpowered the dogs with jets of water, then chained them up. Afterwards, they discovered the caged policemen who were as starved and parched as the dogs were stuffed with food. Order was finally restored, the police station returned to normal, and the dogs were made an example of, as I'm about to explain.

The whole story of the "dogs' revolt" was something I'd read in the paper, like everyone else, in a slew of reports, all of them rife with hyperbole, written by dozens of journalists dispatched to our town by their respective newspapers. But that wasn't what I wanted to talk about, I needed to relate these events to give proper context to something I saw with my own eyes, something that tormented me and disturbed me to the point of hallucination, ruining my moments of rest in a place I thought of as a refuge from the world and where, before all this happened, I would spend hours on end in solitary respite.

As alluded to, the police put all the dogs on trial, and they were sentenced to a public hanging, no doubt to make an example of them and show other dogs the fate that awaited them if they got any ideas into their heads and tried to revolt. And where the public hanging was to take place was none other than the crumbling wall at the edge of town where I would rest in the grass, in the verdant, soothing shade of the immense acacia tree.

So this is how as I was walking one day towards my usual relaxation spot with my journal under my arm, looking forward to a few hours of peace at the end of an exhausting day, I found that lonely place invaded by a large crowd of adults and children, gesticulating, chattering loudly, laughing, shouting, all of them boisterous and excited, talking about the extraordinary spectacle before them — the hanging of the dogs. As I drew closer, I saw the thirty culprits with their eyes bulging out of their sockets, with their tongues lolling out lamentably, as if panting on a hot summer day. They were lined up along the wall, hanging by wooden planks through which ropes were affixed. All the dogs were dressed in their beautiful blue uniforms and police caps, only the S.P. insignia had been ripped off, likely to degrade them, in the same way disgraced soldiers have their medals torn off.

The bodies of the dogs remained there for the next few days, and as they started to rot, a terrible stench filled the air. It was impossible for me to return to that place, so after searching far and wide I found another spot to rest near a riverbank fringed by willows. It's a place I still like to go to. The only thing left to add was that the young ice cream vendor also played a part in this story. One day I saw him pushing his cart down a side street in the company of several policemen. It was his usual cart, decorated with some metal nick-nacks and a plaque proclaiming, *Money — here today, gone tomorrow* written in large red letters, yet this time it was covered in some cheap black cloth, resembling a miniature hearse. I asked some of the people following him what was going on and learned that the policemen had paid the boy to transport the dogs in his ice cream cart to the dog cemetery for burial. This is the detail from that whole story that came back to me, like a vision.

Maybe I should doubt whether these events actually happened or whether I dreamt them, perhaps I should be suspicious of the detailed, perfectly logical way they unfold in my memory. Maybe I ordered them in this rational sequence during my waking hours . . . But whether or not things seem rational has never been of much concern to me ... In fact, I've never cared about it at all. Everything that happens has its own logic, self-created as soon as it unfolds and becomes visible, even if in a dream, just as anything new and original at first seems illogical, even if occurring in reality. Besides, questions such as these never trouble me when I revisit my dreams or memories, whose beauty or oddity enthrals me, with their sad, calm atmosphere or their painful, heart-wrenching drama. Oh, to think of all the deliriously splendid things I've encountered in my dreams, which others will never come close to in all their living days! Because what is most bewildering and exciting is that every ordinary thing is transformed into something ineffable in the world of sleep (or even in reality), something which I cannot then unlearn ... for example, I once saw the square outside the post office in Bucharest in a certain way and after that, both times that I've been driven through it, even with my eyes open, I could only see it as white and red ... that was how it would exist for me eternally.

It was the same square, the same post office framed by columns in front of the Casa de Depuneri bank, the same shops, and the same small park, with people and cars flitting through just as in reality, but all of it, down to the very last detail, was white, completely white. All the cars, all the houses, every leaf, each iron railing, each wisp of the broom that swept the street, the road sweeper himself, all completely white. It was as if all of these things had lost their ordinary forms, the people no longer flesh and blood, the leaves no longer composed of living cells, nor cars of metal, nor houses of bricks, everything moulded instead from curdled milk. Imagine a bottle of milk that suddenly shatters and instead of spilling out the liquid retains its shape. Now, instead of the green bottle, you will see the same form, now a lustrous white. You now have an object that could belong to the square I've been describing.

It was impossible to find even a speck of any other colour. Take, for example, that tall, mustachioed gentleman with a cane, walking slowly in front of the bank and looking up at its clock to adjust the time on his pocket watch. I can see him in the minutest detail, his tiniest gestures, I can see the individual white hairs in his moustache, his alabaster fingers, his pocket watch as milky as porcelain. Its case, springing open, is white, his cane seems to be spun out of sugar just like the bank itself whose architectural details have been nevertheless perfectly preserved, the masonry a matte white while the windows retain their translucence, and the passerby's fleshy cheek and the skin of his hands, just like his skin camouflaged by clothes, are a soft, dull white, like porous, warm putty (because the skin has only changed its tint while keeping its human temperature as well as its pores and all its other organic qualities). All of these details appear so vividly and effortlessly before my eyes that they require no explanation.

But one day something about this vision changed: although everything else was still white, the dome of the bank turned red, extraordinarily red, splendidly red, all the time retaining the glassy sheen of its materials, like a colossal ruby. Then the red from the dome pervaded the whole square as if it were dripping with blood. So to me, that square now always looks either completely white or completely red — white on sunny days when I sit on my terrace facing the garden, but red in the evening when fatigue seals my eyes shut.

I think I prefer to see it bloodstained. When the square is red, the gentleman's whiskers look like shreds of the tissue paper used to pack fragile objects, his waistcoat and jacket make him look like an elegant crab, his cane a cheap stick of candy a child might suck, the windows the lollipops sold by itinerant Turks, the leaves and grass splattered with blood, the liquid spilled from a bottle by a boy is not water but blood — and people's teeth are carved from the finest coral and their fingers from porphyry while their ears are bundles of purple cartilage. When the street sweeper's broom of lobster antennae does its work, the dust billows in a brick-coloured cloud. And the sky arches over us like a gigantic ruby crystal goblet . . .

Most might think this image of the square is snatched out of a dream or my imagination, but one day I came face to face with one of the people I have described, and seeing her in the flesh convinced me that what I had seen was absolutely real. I could have had a conversation with this red creature, if I wanted. All of this happened last summer. It was in the middle of the afternoon and I was sitting on my terrace on a fairly quiet street at the edge of town, watching the world go by. And then a woman from the red piazza appeared. She was dressed in a scarlet silk dress that rustled softly as she walked, matched by a red wide-brimmed hat, wearing red shoes and red stockings, holding a red handbag in her red gloved hands, and her face had a crimson glow.

I could not believe my eyes when I saw this apparition and pointed her out to someone nearby:

"What colour dress is that lady wearing? Her gloves, her dress, her shoes . . . they're all red, aren't they?"

"Exactly," he answered, "it's a bit over the top, but this lady always wears pretty garish outfits, she seems to have a thing for the outlandish . . ."

This was the first time I had seen her. I allowed my interlocutor to believe the lady merely had a flamboyant sense of fashion, but deep down I remained convinced a character from my dream piazza had just appeared to me in the flesh.

Such episodes deeply shook my faith in a stable, coherent reality (a reality I could always embellish with perfectly plausible and convincing modifications whenever I wanted) as well as revealing the essential dreamlike quality of all our everyday actions.

For a long time I would dream of a garden with manicured lawns, classical statues and intricate topiary some truly artistic landscapers must have created by clipping the dense leafage of particular plants. And one day . . .

In summer, I would often ride alone in a carriage through Berck, steering the horse myself. The lonely country roads were my favourites, the hidden lanes that snaked between houses or through woodland. I frequently stopped to chat with the villagers while they worked, so before long I became a familiar face to them, and they greeted me warmly or doffed their caps whenever I rolled through. After all, I was the only patient who would venture to those parts, as the others preferred the beach, their carriages in a circle so they could talk together for hours.

During my jaunts through the countryside I made many discoveries and attracted a number of friends, such as kind, simple housewives who guided my carriage into their yards to show me some newborn bunnies, their muzzles pink and tender like rose petals bejewelled with dew, or a marvellous hen that had laid a bounty of eggs, or other times they would offer me doorstop sandwiches made from their delicious country black bread and filled with honey, cheese and jam, with an extra slice of bacon on top to make them especially tasty with a sweet, salty, meaty combination of flavours I'd never tried before. Another day, the farmer's children brought over to my carriage some owlets they had found in the attic, warm and virtually featherless, like balls of dough that had been rolled in feathers and down. Everyone who approached me was full of good will, enquiring about my health, asking me what the doctor had to say about my condition and how long I would have to remain supine like that.

On one of those outings I discovered the garden from my dream. No one would have guessed that a park like that could exist on the outskirts of Berck, and whenever I came back with my carriage laden with flowers, many still doubted the place I told them about really did exist. Actually, it was rather difficult to find, as it was concealed by a curtain of trees and surrounded by thick, high walls. I had passed it many times and had not guessed the splendour behind those battlements. It was on the edge of a poor village, where sometimes I stopped at a farm that made a special cheese prepared and aged according to an old peasant recipe.

The farmer used to tell me about the "chateau" at the edge of the village where every day he would bring cheese, milk and eggs, but the word "chateau" didn't stir my interest. In the French countryside, any large manor is labelled a chateau and its surrounding yard described as a "park."

Yet one day driving down a side road I hadn't noticed before, I caught a glimpse of this estate through the shrubbery. Not only was the "chateau" surrounded by high walls, but it was also protected by some equally thick and impenetrable hedges, and by sheer chance I noticed a gap which revealed a corner of the garden with a fountain, and beyond it a terrace wreathed with climbing plants and a beautifully crafted wrought-iron gate. An artesian fountain continuously jetted iridescent water, the spray forming a delicate veil over the gate and terrace.

Everything looked so beautiful, so self-possessed and picturesque in that place at the edge of the village that I was overtaken by an irresistible urge to see the inside of the garden. It was like looking through a magic lantern. Chickens were frolicking in the dust of the road, a dirty, shaggy dog had escaped through a fence and was now barking, yet over there, beyond that gap in the hedge, a jet of water soared up from the fountain, curving gracefully into an arch stretched over an elegantly immaculate landscape.

I began searching for the entrance. Yet the gate must have long been buried behind the hedges and I couldn't find it, all I could do was to wander around the surrounding walls. I managed to find an iron gate, rusty, old, and suffocated by ivy, all boarded up to prevent anyone from entering.

I waited outside for a few moments, thinking that someone might come out or try to go in, but the complete stillness of the place suggested I could have waited hours for nothing. I decided to knock, trying to concoct a pretext for my visit. Voices could be heard from behind the gate, followed by a hushed conversation, then someone peered through the bars and without opening the gate asked gruffly:

"What do you want?"

At that moment, my mind went blank.

"I'd like to speak with the owner of this chateau . . ."

After a couple of minutes of hesitation and more whispers, the gate finally creaked open and a chubby man with glowing red cheeks appeared in the doorway, puffing and out of breath. He wore a blue apron over a cheap velvet jacket.

"The owner is away at the moment . . . he won't be back for a month . . . the gardener and I are the only ones here . . . is it something urgent?"

The owner's absence was very convenient, because now I could make up any excuse for being there without anyone to contradict me.

"I have something very important to tell him . . . a message from one of his oldest, closest friends . . . but I can only give it to him."

As I was speaking, my eyes were greedily drinking in the vision behind the gate. It was just as beautiful as it seemed when I glimpsed it through the bushes, only even more breathtaking. A long terrace supported by stone columns curved around the right side of the garden. It was filled with flowers.

"You have such beautiful flowers here!" I exclaimed. "Only a true expert could grow them out of this sandy soil . . . You don't see flowers like this anywhere around here, unless you travel for dozens of kilometres inland . . ."

As I was saying this, the gardener drew closer to my carriage. He was a tall, withered old man with sunken cheeks and a shock of white hair like a wooly fleece, snowy whiskers, bushy eyebrows and a red-tipped nose like a tender rosebud ready to bloom . . . I could tell by the satisfied and slightly vain smile hiding behind those whiskers that he was flattered by my praise.

"But you can barely see anything from over there . . . ," he said.

"Who is this gentleman?" the gardener asked his short, chubby colleague.

"He's looking for the master . . . he has a message for him, from a friend."

After the gardener asked me some questions about who I was, if I was staying in Berck and the nature of my illness, he pulled the other man aside and they whispered together for a few seconds. I could tell they had come to some sort of agreement because the portly fellow who had initially seemed quite hostile smiled at me and nodded approvingly.

"Alright, we might as well let him in," he announced loudly. And then, walking towards me:

"Seeing as you're interested in our flowers, the gardener would like to show you around, if you can bring your carriage inside the courtyard, or if you could manage to get out and walk with us . . ."

Although I was not able to get out, I was more than happy to steer my carriage inside, as this was exactly the invitation I had been waiting for! They opened the gate wide and the care-taker took hold of the reins and led the horse into the yard. I made my way towards the terrace and noticed that it was cov-ered with fine, rust coloured pebbles. It rose above the garden and to reach it you had to climb an imposing stone staircase with large, polished steps, framed by urns painted in pastel colours and overflowing with exotic foliage that poured down like russet-gold lace. The colours of the plants were matched to the urns, and the stone columns at the top and bottom of the staircase supported the largest pots, almost the size of wine barrels. It was, without question, the most magnificent and harmonious thing I'd ever seen! The cobalt blue urns were lavishly fringed with lemon foliage, and the contrast between that deep blue and vivid yellow created a vision of unspeakable exquisiteness and charm. But this was only the first of the wonderful things I would encounter.

Wherever I looked, my eyes filled with hues and shapes of unparalleled beauty. At the end of a path edged with white roses I glimpsed the "chateau's" entrance, to the side of where I had stopped my carriage by the terrace. It was an old-fashioned door with wrought-iron embellishments and tiny stained-glass windows of the kind that used to be crafted in France hundreds of years ago. Apart from this, nothing else about the building itself seemed old fashioned.

The rest of the park stretched beyond the terrace, but my carriage would not manage to make it through there. Still, I could see the statues surrounded by carefully manicured hedges, I could see the fountain at its centre and the tiny waterfalls gushing crystal water through the rocks and mountains of flowers. It was the garden I had visited many times in my dreams, and I was not the least bit surprised to find it again here, looking the same as always . . . Everything I saw stirred in me the kind of nostalgia that lingers after a broken dream you awake from cloaked in a sadness borrowed from those beautiful, forlorn places you have wandered, the melancholy emptiness of astonishing gardens, the enchantment of the footpaths you have trod without encountering another soul . . .

I returned many times to that "chateau" and became ever closer to its attendants. One time, they lifted me out of the carriage and carried me as if on a stretcher down the staircase towards a sheltered spot in the park where I could have a panoramic view of the whole place and spend a few hours of uninterrupted bliss. It was nearly autumn and the garden was fading. The wind twirled reels of golden leaves dappled with blood and rust along the alleys. During those moments, the austere garden and crystalline murmur of the waterfalls melded into a sombre, endless solitude . . .

When I returned to the sanatorium and took my place at the communal dining table, everything seemed insipid, desolate and stale. The way the pots of exotic plants in the corners of the hall vainly paraded their extravagant foliage seemed a bit pathetic to me.

"You've seemed preoccupied the past few days," a woman at my table remarked. "When I speak to you . . . you're looking straight at me, but you don't hear me . . . nothing seems to register . . ."

I had brought her flowers and told her where they had come from, but preferred to hold back, like a secret pleasure, everything I'd seen and experienced in the garden of the "chateau."

I was informed by the estate's staff that the owner was expected back shortly and on what day I should return so that I could finally deliver to him the message from his close friend. Since I wasn't sure what type of man he was and feared he wouldn't understand my true motives, I decided to avoid the garden altogether. I'm sure the gardener and the caretaker must have been surprised by my vanishing act that coincided with their master's return.

But how could anyone have understood that all I wanted was to visit the garden I had glimpsed in a dream, each night wandering its splendid, deserted paths, losing myself in a silence simmering with the murmur of waterfalls, reliving again and again the wonder of my solitary days?

The memory of it alone was enough . . . but the following spring I couldn't resist trying to catch a glimpse of the fountain through the opening in the hedges on the road near the chateau. Yet the circumstances that brought me there were too sad and painful for this reunion to bring me any joy. I will tell you more about that portentous day, because this dramatic episode in my life as a patient made such a profound impression on me that even now when I recall it, I feel that deeply buried angst starting to stir.

On rainy autumn days, the sanatorium patients would sit in a line on a terrace, with a view to the garden and an imposing ornate hotel further beyond. The days were sodden, waterlogged, drowning in rain, ravished by wind and hooded by clouds perpetually drifting in from the ocean, thin, hazy, ashen stains on an ashen sky, scattering inland like birds of smoke.

Behind the hotel, the chimney of a factory kept belching out smog, so that the hotel with its rows of small windows extended out of this murk like a ship moored in rain, ready to weigh anchor.

The gate at the bottom of the alley leading to the road was always open, and occasionally some shaggy, scrawny dog, its fur drenched and mottled by rain, would wander in to sniff around the bushes and the faux antique columns where he would stop at a carefully selected spot, lift up his leg and add his own thin spray to the deluge of water pouring from the sky.

Wrapped in blankets neck high, the patients were "taking the air," their teeth chattering from the cold. They couldn't read, as their hands were under the blankets to keep warm, so they chatted quietly instead, engaging in long conversations about matters that would never mean anything to them in their "recumbent" state or while immobilised in plaster casts.

Some of them were talking about horse races, others about

"aviation," an especially popular topic of conversation, and it was quite interesting listening to the extremely well-informed opinions, worthy of engineers, formulated through meticulous study of specialist journals that filled the rooms of these would-be aviators imprisoned in plaster casts. They, of course, regarded me as an ignoramus with no serious preoccupations. One of the young men I befriended on the terrace was constantly astounded by how clueless I was:

"How is it possible, sir, that you have no interest in this new mode of transport that will connect places the world over and reduce the distance between them to nothing?"

I couldn't suppress an amused smile as I recognised, word for word, the information found in myriad newspaper articles. He was a cheerful lad, with large brown eyes and jet black hair with an almost bluish sheen, and his hands were pale and slender, the hands of a sick man, but also the hands of an artist. The thing I liked best about him was that he used to sketch, and there was something refined about his manner, something that betrayed an artistic temperament.

I remember a couple of instances that illustrated his sensibilities and his inquiring spirit. One day, I wanted to give him a present, so I took him into town and gave him the choice between a children's book with coloured pictures of animals and a book of fables with fewer, but more elaborate illustrations, real works of art, printed on exquisite paper. He chose the latter, explaining: "This one is the work of a master, you can see that these are copperplate prints made by someone with real skill, vastly superior to these garish drawings mass printed in seconds by a machine . . . one after another . . ." He accompanied these last words with a comical whirling of his hands as if to demonstrate the heedless rush with which the printing press had churned out the coloured pages.

I also remember an encounter with him in the waiting room of the sanatorium. We were both lying on our gurneys when I pulled out a packet of foreign cigarettes from underneath my pillow.

"It's exactly the same shade as the wall!" my little friend exclaimed.

It was true, the pink box was amazingly similar to the shade of the wallpaper. It was only a small detail, but I hadn't noticed it until then, despite the fact that I had taken cigarettes from the packet many times in the waiting room. That my friend had noticed this was surely proof of an artistic sensibility and how his inner world worked, similar to the way a machine is programmed to sort objects of identical sizes.

I called him Boby, as did everyone else in the sanatorium, but if anyone asked him his name he would introduce himself solemnly as Robert Vanderkich, from Belgium, but using an emphatic Flemish pronunciation in case anyone made the mistake of thinking he was just an ordinary Belgian, and then he would shake his mane of hair with a triumphant flourish.

A few days ago, I found amongst my papers a pencil sketch he'd made, a rough portrait of me. I was taken aback by the fact that I hadn't recognised his skill at the time, this boy with no formal art training. True, he had not rendered my features precisely and his technique was far from flawless, but overall the composition had a power that went beyond the idle doodles of a child having fun with a piece of paper. And this was not just my opinion, it was also confirmed by experts, professional artists, who studied the sketch and were amazed when I told them the artist's age.

I regret I could never make a reproduction of this sketch for the simple reason that he drew everything on pages torn from diaries his aunt used to bring him from Paris. Bought in a department store, they had lined pages divided into columns like a ledger. The pages still had enough blank space for Boby to draw on, but the column lines or the name of some brand advertised in the diary marred each sketch, so in addition to Robert Vanderkich's signature, my portrait also contained an advert for bedding that spanned the whole length of my forehead.

He was very ill, one of his knees was so damaged the leg had to stay raised at all times, his body was covered in fistulas, which must have been terrible for such a young boy like him, and his genitals were wrapped in a bulky bandage, which, as I later learned, made him the butt of cruel, juvenile jokes by his thoughtless roommates in the dormitory.

Whenever the porters came to take Boby to have his bandages changed, he always pretended to be busy and begged them to wait a few minutes or to take someone else first, and when he realised there was no escape, he would pack up his books and paper in resignation, muttering *merde!* under his breath with a grimness beyond his years, and then announce he was ready to go.

Occasionally we were taken to have our bandages changed at the same time, but he always swung it so that I would go in first. But one time, he went in first, and as I was lying on my gurney just outside the door, I realised the agonies the boy was forced to endure every day. I heard him screaming, grunting and weeping wildly, his howls at times so desperate they seemed the last gasp of breath he would ever take. At certain moments, the dreadful electric bell would loudly go off, and its sinister clangour mingling with the screams inside the room made me feel I was in a house of horrors where the condemned were systematically tortured in antiseptic rooms by nurses clad in white aprons and doctors with rubber gloves pulled up to their elbows.

That afternoon I asked him what all the screaming was about.

"What are they doing in there? Trying to kill you? You're a grown lad, you should be ashamed of making such a racket when they're just changing your bandages . . ."

But I regretted my words immediately.

"I try to stay quiet," he answered, "but I can't do it, I feel I'm going mad . . . what can I say? They're dousing my balls with pure ether."

And he said this in a way that was so serious and mature, as if he knew there was no shame in admitting such things.

That autumn his condition worsened, he was called to the clinic more frequently, and retired to the dormitory around five with a high fever, unable to endure sunlight any longer. While all his young friends cavorted noisily outside and raced around on their wheelchairs, he would shutter himself in the semi-darkness of the dormitory, curtains drawn, alone and trembling with fever, his cheeks ablaze and hands frozen, shivering and sweating, ice cold and then boiling hot, listening, in a daze, his head simmering with heat, to the squeals of joy and conversations of his friends that echoed from the terrace where they played until dinnertime.

One day the doctor decided that Boby needed an operation and sent a telegram to his father. When he arrived, the boy was summoned for another checkup, and it was decided the surgery would take place in a few days. Until that day arrived, the father took his son out for a walk every morning, "to the beach and back," pushing the wheelchair himself. When they returned, if there was still time before lunch, they sat on the terrace with the other patients. On the very first day of this new routine, Boby eagerly introduced me to his father. As it turned out, he had often mentioned me and our friendship to him, and the man thanked me for taking an interest in his son. I was a little bewildered and explained that I thought Boby was a bright, talented boy and that I thoroughly enjoyed our conversations. He was extremely flattered and couldn't stop grinning, revealing a gappy set of teeth with a few tobacco-yellowed stumps sunk deep in his gums.

He was a farmer, a robust, broad-shouldered man with grey hair and white moustache, with a solid neck, red and full of small folds as if cut by a knife, the fleshy neck of a powerful animal, reared in the bracing country air that had weathered his skin. When he was standing, our wheelchairs only came up

/ 48 /

to his stomach, and when he pushed his son, his thick, calloused hands gripping the handles, it seemed like the easiest thing in the world to him, accustomed as he was to wielding heavier tools in his fields. He was constantly smoking thick yellow cigarettes of ordinary tobacco rolled in special "maize paper," and when he exhaled, the smoke looked as if it did not come only out of his nose, but out of his ears and neck too, veiling his whole head in a cloud.

The day before the operation, Boby was taken to a room adjacent to the clinic. He said goodbye to me with a certain sadness, but gave no indication he was aware how serious the procedure was, about which the doctor had already warned his father. On the day of the operation, I didn't see his father at all. He was probably sitting in one of those "private rooms" with their enigmatic closed doors, completely isolated, both spatially and spiritually, from the normal life of the sanatorium. A few days later, I found out from a nurse that Boby's operation had been successful, but he wasn't well. This was the usual diplomatic yet ludicrous understatement you would hear in the hospital when someone was on their last legs.

Mr. Vanderkich finally approached me in the corridor one afternoon. He seemed miserable and agitated. He told me right away that Boby had suffered a haemorrhage "down there" and had lost too much blood to carry on fighting the illness. His fever wouldn't go down and the bandages cut into his flesh so painfully that Boby didn't even have the energy to scream. He was exhausted and paralysed by his agony. His eyes stayed shut, he'd just let rivulets of saliva run down his chin and squeak like a mouse the whole time. Worse still, one time he wet the bed . . .

These facts escaped Mr. Vanderkich's lips in a frantic jumble — clearly he had an urgent need to confide in someone but was also in a great hurry. Right then he was waiting for the doctor to come out of a patient's room so he could tell him that the man who was going to donate blood for Boby's transfusion had left town to the countryside for a few days, so where did that now leave them?

"Where did you say he was staying?" the doctor asked, and Mr. Vanderkich told him the name of the village.

"Well, that's not far," the doctor replied, "you can make it there in an hour if you take the carriage and I'm sure this gentleman will show you the way," he added, pointing at me.

"Of course!" I exclaimed. "We"ll leave now and have the man here by lunchtime."

At that moment I remembered this was the village with the "chateau" I last visited several weeks ago, since I'd been trying to avoid its owner. There was a good chance I would bump into the caretaker or the gardener in the village, which would be awkward. But my potential embarrassment was far outweighed by the emergency that compelled us to go there! I smothered my momentary hesitation in an avalanche of self-reproach . . .

Mr. Vanderkich took a seat beside me in the carriage, lit one of his thick cigarettes, and began puffing away heartily. His weary eyes, sunken by so many sleepless nights watching over his son, stared, distracted, at the fields, and he only occasionally broke his tense silence to remark on the state of the harvest or some other agricultural matter. Sometimes in life depression creates such a distraction that common, everyday concerns burst through it without warning. More than once I turned my head to look at him and marvelled at his robust health, the same question fluttering on my lips: Why didn't he donate the blood to his son?

He stared at me for a long time and then lit another cigarette, but did not reply, almost as if he hadn't understood the question. When at last he answered, I realised his silence had only been reticence.

"Yes, it's true, I could have given him blood . . . but you see . . . there's a sad story here . . ."

At that precise moment we came to the village and a child greeted us and asked what house we were looking for. I was dying to hear the "sad story" that prevented Mr. Vanderkich from donating blood to his own child, but there was no time to ask anymore questions. We were actually very close to the address we wanted and by the time we got there, Mr. Vanderkich was practically trembling with impatience. He jumped out the carriage even before we even reached the house and with gigantic strides, like a huge animal, bounded to the door in seconds and pounded on it violently.

An old lady in a black shawl around her shoulders opened the door.

"Can I help you?"

Mr. Vanderkich quickly explained the situation.

"I'm afraid it's a waste of time," the old woman replied. "I'm sorry you had to come all this way for nothing . . . The man you're looking for is my son, but he caught the flu and came here from Berck so I could look after him until he's better. You can come in and see him if you like, he's in bed, I'll go and see if he's awake."

"We shouldn't disturb him," muttered Mr. Vanderkich. "It's pointless . . . we'll go . . . my apologies . . . there's nothing for us here . . ."

Just as we were about to leave, the old lady called me over and told me about a shortcut through a nearby street. It was the street from where I had first glimpsed the chateau through the hedges.

Yet as I traversed it again, my mind was consumed by completely different thoughts and feelings than the ones I had experienced several weeks earlier, and my agitation prevented me from enjoying my memories of the place.

Sitting next to me in the carriage, Mr. Vanderkich kept mumbling and lamenting:

"What do I do now? He was the only one in the whole of Berck who could have given him blood. And now he's sick . . . And the clock is ticking . . . and Boby is getting worse and worse . . . and I can't do anything but stand by and watch it happen, with my hands tied, powerless to do a thing . . . That's the most painful thing, knowing you could've helped someone, your own child, but some completely stupid twist of fate has made it all impossible . . ."

He wiped his face with a hand, then took out a blue polka-dotted handkerchief and dabbed his eyes. Yes, he was crying, and it was all the more painful to see such a giant of a man, broad-shouldered and neck like an ox, weeping like a child.

At last he calmed down and between sighs told me the cause of his despair.

"I told you it was a sad story — well, it's more stupid than sad. I'm sure you know that during the war some regiments were posted to the Eastern Front. I was a corporal in one such regiment stationed somewhere near Thessaloniki, right up to the Armistice — what a great time we had! But it was exactly all this fun that landed me in trouble, because we had plenty of money and got drunk like pigs and then partied in brothels till morning . . . In one of those brothels I caught a disease, and it's still with me . . . ah! One drunken night of lovemaking stained the rest of my entire life, my blood became forever "tainted." When I returned home, Boby was three and barely recognised me because when I'd left he was only a few months old and still breastfeeding . . . And now I'd come back to him and couldn't even give him a kiss . . . now it's even worse, he's dying and I can't help him."

He wiped his face again with his hand and then retreated into himself, falling silent and sinking deeper into thought, sighing from time to time.

The doctor seemed very concerned that we hadn't managed to bring the blood donor with us.

"It's an urgent matter, you see, very urgent," he kept repeating to the farmer, who could only stare at him, dewy-eyed and speechless.

In the end, having heard that a blood donation was

necessary, the wife of one of the patients offered to do it. She was a nurse at a hospital in Paris and had given blood before.

They gave Boby the transfusion that same afternoon and he started to feel better . . .

And that's how he died later that night, with his agonies allayed and blissfully at peace.

I still have the picture he drew for me, and, in a way, the memory of seeing the "chateau" again the day he died filled me with such nostalgia and sadness that I could never ever go back to that village.

All the thoughts, all the memories, all the visions I've ever experienced disappear and sink on the other side of my eyelids into the warm darkness inside the skin, the darkness which absorbs them completely. Coddled inside this gentle heat and that nameless intimate space, they are indistinct, merging into one another, all the memories, all the feelings, everything that has ever meant anything in my life. Even as a specific memory is recalled, it has no greater value or significance to distinguish it from any other. Everything that once seemed so momentous and dramatic eventually fades, turns pale, anaemic, as it lies dormant in memory, the echoes of a vague sorrow shifting it towards banality, while all the trivial things memory initially rejected as insignificant in the moment they happened now shine brightly, suddenly transformed into extraordinary revelations.

I have only one way of explaining it: we create our lives each moment through our imagination, and in that instant life makes sense, but only in that moment and only in the way our imagination contrives it. Yes, living and dreaming are one and the same. Everything we dream seems true at the time, its reality tied to those nocturnal hours of sleep, in the same way that we live out our days, when our thoughts and actions appear irrefutably real although they too are spawned by our imagination. But even if we persuade ourselves that such a thing as objective reality exists independent of our meddling minds, it's enough to just close our eyes when faced with a tragedy and retreat within ourselves to find a narrow, hermetic inner world, free from all else, and discover that any memory can still be fished out of that darkness, any thought or image we might choose, that even in the midst of this tragedy we might remember a joke, an anecdote, the title of a book, or the plot of a movie.

In my waking hours, whenever I was having a serious discussion and felt as though my full attention were engaged, my mind would start to wander and imagine an entirely new conversation, completely different and bizarre, sometimes fantastical, sometimes amusing, while my face retained the same serious expression . . .

I actually remember when being told on different occasions about a particularly gory and gruesome death, the most eccentric troupe of little rubber animals would "involuntarily" appear on the stage of the small, private theatre inside my mind, performing cartoon dances, acrobatics, and astounding leaps, a spectacle entertaining, extraordinary, and truly hilarious. All the while I furrowed my brow and listened with a compassionate expression. Think of all the secret things hidden inside each person we talk to!

The essence of reality is, after all, a farrago of random details without meaning or significance. Even if external appearances seem clearly defined, the motifs are often confused, as the setting and the characters who have their parts to play are confused without adequate illumination. A grave, melancholy character is played by a mediocre actor who can barely remember his lines and — even worse — feels ill at ease in his role.

The sanatorium cared for sick men and especially sick women who seemed to have been there since the beginning of the world, for whom the secret powers of the universe had reserved a static life of suffering, a fate of resignation. I knew an older girl, for instance, who with her brother had been involved in a car accident which sentenced her to a lifetime of terrible illness and the torment of bone tuberculosis in both of her knees. Her skin was sallow, her hair black and lank, her hands slender and anaemic, and her eyes wore a placid, moist look like that of a domesticated animal. She would bring a book of litanies to the dining hall and bury her head in it between courses. Well, one could only conclude that the "accident" had somehow been by the design of a higher power, as it so happened her brother came out of it unscathed in mind and body while she was the one who had to suffer, and being pious, she accepted her suffering like a martyr. And in case anyone thought her wan melancholy a consequence of the accident, her brother was quick to disabuse them of this notion if you ever caught a quiet word with him in the garden, in his sister's absence, of course:

"She's always been like that . . . as long as I've known her.

She used to lie in bed all day with a headache and her nose stuck in a prayer book . . . she's no different than before . . . the illness hasn't changed her at all, I can assure you, she even still wears all those medallions around her neck . . ."

There were of course exceptions, and they seemed to me the most fascinating and impressive.

All sorts of lives and stories inhabited the sanatorium. When I leaf through an old photo album and find a snapshot of a splendid summer afternoon in the garden, my mind is flooded by thousands of pangs and dramas breezily concealed beneath a smile beaming at me from the shade of a grove in bloom. Look, it's Teddy with her movie-star smile, striking a rebellious pose on her stretcher! Petite, pretty and snub-nosed, with the fantastic Parisian accent of a girl who knew how to have a good time in a big city. There she lay in the same clothes she would wear when healthy. She was the only woman who would show up in the dining hall in a tailored outfit, with a short skirt and silk stockings, causing the old ladies to whisper amongst themselves about how "indecent" she looked with her legs hoisted up on the gurney. They got used to her as time went on, and after a while didn't even raise an eyebrow when she would order a filtered coffee after dinner and light up a cork-tipped Craven A cigarette.

She was a refined little minx, a petite Parisian girl who had turned many a head before she fell ill.

After we became friends, she used to regale me with stories of her romantic adventures. On certain days of the month she would wait for the post in a state of agitation and asked me to check in the newspaper — she never bought one herself — when the mail ships from Dakar were due to arrive. A few times I noticed on her table envelopes with West African stamps, but the thing that struck me as strange was that they were all addressed to Miss Teddy Pelisier, Poste Restante, Paris, at some suburban post office.

One day I asked her who sent those letters, and she answered directly that they were from "her little lover" who had moved to the colonies before her illness and still knew nothing of her condition or that she was at Berck, so he continued to write her at the usual address. Her sister picked up the letters and forwarded them to the sanatorium. She told me he was a young engineer who had asked her to marry him before he left, and he was planning to stay in the colonies for a few years to make his fortune and then build a life back at home. In the photographs of them together her dresses moulded perfectly around her slender body, while he looked serious, a pipe hanging from his lips, gazing at her admiringly, his arm gently circling her waist. The pictures were taken in front of the casino in Deauville and in various parks in Belgian towns — they both had relatives in Belgium and would dutifully visit them together, like a nice, respectable, perfectly matched betrothed couple.

During those afternoons when we would sit in her room and look at the photo album together, we were often interrupted by a knock on the door as the nurse came to take her temperature, and it felt truly unjust that my eyes should fall on a photo of Teddy in a white sailor dress on the deck of a boat sailing towards some Balearic island just as she was tucking the thermometer under her arm like any other invalid and then confessing to the grey-eyed, downy lipped nurse who was standing in the middle of the room as impassive as a vegetable that it read 38.1 °C but she felt fine, so that I wouldn't be asked to leave.

It was horribly unjust that this creature destined for a life of pleasure and caresses should lie amidst prostrate, neurasthenic, sombre bodies in the corridor of a sanatorium, lost among the sand dunes at the edge of the ocean, in a solitude and isolation that not only tortured her but shook the foundations of her reality.

One day her sister forwarded to the sanatorium an enormous box from Dakar filled with the skins of many small wild animals. I remember a bed cover made of four hides diagonally stitched together, two of which I identified as antelope and another two I didn't recognise, some kind of soft, velvety fur striped like that of a tiger. When I came to see her that afternoon, I expected to find her happy about the gift, but found her crying instead. She'd been in tears since coming up from the dining hall, she told me, because of her situation, because he didn't know anything about her illness, while she lay on a gurney with a high fever. And as she uttered the word "gurney," she pounded the mattress and ground her teeth.

"You'll get better, Teddy. By the time he returns you'll be back on your feet and you'll welcome his boat in Bordeaux with a big smile on your face, as if nothing had happened."

In truth, her illness was more advanced than she realised. In addition to the damaged vertebrae, the doctors also found a large quantity of albumin in her urine, which indicated kidney problems, a serious complication that meant she had to cut salt from her diet and give up her after dinner filtered coffee. She lost an awful lot of weight over the next few months. One day when her sister came to visit, she was told by the doctor that one of Teddy's kidneys would have to be removed.

That afternoon we all went to the cinema. The cinemas in Berck all had wooden benches at the back where the stretchers of the patients could be placed. It must have looked strange to anyone who saw this arrangement for the first time: half of the room seated on chairs, the other half lying on stretchers. When the lights went down, the waves of blurred reality that filled the screen veiled our supine bodies in a strange luminous pallor, as if half of the audience was made up of embalmed corpses lying in sarcophagi inside some kind of museum in the middle of the night.

I was lying next to Teddy, who had been informed about the operation that morning and decided to come to the cinema to escape her dark thoughts. When it was time to dim the lights she seemed cheerful, or at least indifferent, but about half way through the film I noticed she was crying quietly in the dark. The glow of the screen intensified the gauntness of her cheeks and transformed her into a stranger. A mix of tears and mascara ran down in dark rivulets, creating two bizarre black lines on a plaster death mask, like a strange funeral tattoo made with charcoal, similar to the burial rites of primitive tribes I've seen in photographs.

She did her best to wipe her eyes before the film ended, but for the next few days she looked sad. Something else happened that made the whole situation significantly worse. The unforeseen has a kind of magnetic force that gravitates towards painful events and serious complications. Her engineer beau wrote her a long letter to announce he'd been given a two-month leave and naturally would be spending it with his fiancée in France.

Downcast, Teddy showed me the letter.

"I thought I could spare him the nasty surprise and now I only have bitter sorrow to offer him instead of joy . . ."

I spent a few days with her after the operation, and then she was transferred to another sanatorium near Paris where she died because she couldn't keep down any food, because her remaining kidney had become infected and not — as the doctors categorically assured us — as a result of the operation, which had been an unqualified success. The medical profession of late has tended towards these types of special explanations that are not quite sophistry nor paradoxical but have a self-contained logic that falls under the category of "regrettable consequences." While such explanations might be convenient since they hold up under logical and ethical scrutiny, they are absolutely useless to patients and their parents.

When I saw Teddy in the sanatorium, she was lying on a special "Dupont" bed that took up most of the room. In fact, they had to get rid of a lot of her things to make space for the enormous bed with its pipes and nickel-plated bars. It was a huge machine in the middle of a bare room that had been emptied just so it would fit, a loom laden not with bolts of cloth but with the white, fragile bed that held the body of a sick woman. There were handles and screws you could press and turn to manoeuvre it. When they changed her bandages or washed her, the bed was raised up using levers and ropes, and a few straps could be untied underneath to release different parts of the body.

"What a complicated business my death has become . . . ," Teddy weakly remarked, and the clarity with which she understood her condition horrified me.

"It's better this way," she added, "much better . . . much better that my fiancé should mourn at my grave than pity an invalid."

All true, it was better this way.

For Teddy, it was an ending that somehow straightened things out and untangled the confusion of roles and motifs that reality had muddled over the course of her life.

Quiet and pale, she lies with her hands neatly folded on her chest, in a large and beautiful suburban Paris cemetery that I have only glimpsed through the misted window of an ambulance, the girl that should have lived and loved, and no-one will know of that hollow-eyed skeleton that replaced her a few days before her death.

Under a fine, cold rain, in an immaculate cemetery, an engineer in a raincoat will place a bouquet of flowers, carefully wrapped to keep them dry, on a simple, neat gravestone that will never reveal anything to anyone, ever.

And in a room a few exotic furs will remain scattered on a

sofa, and still hidden away in a closet will be a photo album and a locked box full of envelopes with stamps from faraway Dakar.

Meanwhile, new patients will come to Berck in search of health, filing in like skeletons with glum, bitter smiles, with their cares and their paralysis and their bandages and their families and their pains and their pus.

Teddy was right, I think, when she said it was better that way.

II

SOMETIMES WHEN I CLOSE MY EYES I CAN CALL UP A particular memory from amongst all the others and feel it come to life with the intensity of its bygone reality, or other times my head is filled with places and events that never existed but which possess the same intensity and absolute light as if they did, and then I open my eyes to the sunny afternoon and see, gushing out like artesian fountains, the colours and shapes of the day, the fine, feathery green of the grass, the dahlias, a lustrous yellow like Chinese silk, the baby blue of the forget-me-nots that calls out to the smooth, deep blue of the sky, so deep and so smooth that its mystery envelops my brain in a fog of lucid drowsiness. When memories, visions and places dance underneath my eyelids, I often wonder, touched by it all, what is the meaning of this endless inner light and how much of the world does it comprise, and the inexorable answer always pains me . . .

The heart of reality is so unfathomable and of such great magnitude and grandiose diversity that our imagination is only able to extract a tiny fraction, enough to glean a few lights and interpretations to weave its "thread of life." And like a delicate, infinite wisp of light and reverie, this thread of life ties every being to the exterior reservoir of a reality filled with places and events, with life and dream, just like an infant blindly pressing lips to a mother's breast and sucking her warm, nourishing milk.

Lying within the time that has not yet drained away are all the adventures, feelings, thoughts and fantasies waiting to come into being, to gradually be distributed amongst future generations who will claim their share of this reality, with all its dreams and madness. The world's immense reservoir of madness will feed so many dreamers! The world's immense reservoir of reverie will spawn so many poems, and its immense reservoir of nocturnal dreams will populate so many of the slumbering with nightmares and terrors! They all lie in wait, dark and astonishing, inside the storeroom of an unknown reality. Heaped together inside the vastness of time, they unfold slowly, cell by cell, fibre by fibre, dream by dream, composing each moment like a mosaic, in every corner of the world, piece by piece, until they form that unimaginable, ever-evolving tableau of "universal life." And this realisation only strikes me during a single moment of my life, the moment when I write, as I feel my blood coursing through obscure channels, in serpentine, living streams, digging its way through dark flesh, connecting nerves to bones, its low, pulsating murmur drowning in the body's night.

It flows in the darkness like a network of rivers, through

thousands and thousands of tributaries, and if I imagine that I'm small enough to float on a raft through one of the arteries, my head fills with a liquid roar while underneath it I hear the beat of my pulse like a gong, reverberating deeper under the skin by the swelling waves while I'm cast further into the gloom and fall into the thunderous cascades of the heart, into cellars constructed of muscle and sinew, immense reservoirs that fill with blood for an instant before the sluices open and it gushes out again with a terrible convulsion, as if the walls of my own room had contracted and squeezed out all the air, and then the blood, invigorated by this assault, thickens, cell by cell, and rushes through the soft, slick canals like a river plunging into obscurity.

In the darkness, I plunge my arm up to the elbow in the river carrying me, and its waters are warm, steamy, astonishingly fragrant. I cup my hands and bring the warm liquid to my lips, and its saltiness reminds me of the taste of tears and the ocean. Darkness, I am locked in the roar and steam of my own blood. And then I think of all those obscure rivers, cascades and rivulets of blood buried inside so many people on this earth, I think of those dark unbridled deluges beneath the skin while they walk or sleep, I think of all those creatures with arteries and veins, the animals that possess the same heat within their flesh, the same steaming, roaring blood.

And when I try to conjure up an image of all the blood in this world, I imagine people and animals stripped of their flesh, nerves and bones leaving only a network of arteries and veins, retaining the shape of the vanished bodies but having a life of its own, like a fine scarlet web of humans and beasts spun from fibres, roots and vines instead of heavy flesh, but still resembling their human form, with heads like hollow balls knitted from yarn of blood, noses straight or aquiline moulded out of delicate webs, lips a red mesh that opens and closes, and when the wind blows, they tremble like dry leaves in an autumn breeze.

And these fleshless bodies, these networks of fibres and arteries, are out there now, all over the world, circulating, sleeping and eating like ordinary people, walking amongst the leaves, grass and trees, a sanguine vegetal army amidst a land of sap and chlorophyll. A world of pure blood, a world of arterial beings and fibrous bodies, a world that is no figment of my imagination, but exists in reality, underneath the skins of all people and animals, present right at the moment I think and write about it: the world or reality that lies under the skin, under the forms and light we see when we open our eyes.

This is how my mind perceives the world of blood, and I realise I'm only an insignificant tangle of threads and arteries amongst a forest of arterial, sanguinary trees, and that the murmur of my blood as it rustles in my veins is only a feeble vibration within the earth's clamorous symphony of blood. And the restless wind, the crashing waves, the roaring rivers drown out the rustle of my blood until it dissolves in a sea of noise. Oh! The monstrous clamour of our planet suspended in space! And amongst all this clamour, the faint murmur of my blood! Swallowed up entirely, entirely insignificant!

And then a new thought terrifies me.

While I am writing, while the pen races across the page shaping words out of lines and curves, words that incredibly (because for me, writing is a profoundly incomprehensible, astounding process) will hold some meaning for those unknown others who will read them, while I sit here writing these lines, something is shifting in every atom of space. In the garden a bird has flown from one branch to another, a leaf trembled in the breeze, a pram with a slightly creaky wheel crossed the street, a baby wailed, a sharp instrument penetrated a solid body, a labourer on the other side of the road hammered a piece of wood, a cow lowed long, an unidentifiable muffled noise escaped from a neighbour's barn, in the garden next door someone shakes the tree waiting for the ripe fruit to fall, the screech of a violin competes with the bark of a dog in a back-street, and then I have to stop, because I can't keep track of the countless things that are happening all around me.

Then I think of everything unfolding just outside the action in my field of vision and the movements, sights and sounds frantically multiply, as in every street things are happening con-stantly, more than I could guess, horrifyingly more. How much more? A terrifying number, countless gestures and actions, peo-ple talking while others smoke, while some sip their tea in cafés and others dream in their slumber or gently brush the dust off their coats, and horses are hitched to carriages at the same time a film plays in a dark cinema and the steam rises in the public baths and the trains glide on their tracks and the wind stirs through everything, ravishing forests, and the rivers continue to race on, flinging wooden rafts from vertiginous heights . . .

Things are happening in the world this very moment as I write, so many things and so many events that all the words that have ever been uttered since the world began and all the words that are still to be spoken in the future would not be enough to describe all that occurs in a single instant. Every moment of my life, every move I've made, every pain I've felt, everything I've experienced, including those things that seemed so extraordinary to me, are only an atom lost in the vast ocean of world events.

And my life is only another speck in this perfectly amorphous and indistinct paste of world events.

Every life is surrounded by this wasteland of world deeds that never cease to multiply, sentenced to solitude amidst a desert filled with action. When I consider this, when I think about the murmur of my blood that hides like a curtain of whispers, the murmur of the entire world, and I reflect on my life, adrift amidst so many others, it seems to me that everything I do or write is futile, that the visions illuminating my mind dissipate in this immense multitude, just as somewhere the phosphorescence of a tranquil sea is engulfed by the darkness of night while the wind rests and the starry sky covers the vastness of the tropical ocean in its vault of silence. And the lines and phrases I pen are also just glimmers of phosphorescence, senselessly, eternally vanished into the night . . .

Before I fell ill, I thought all my actions had a purpose, that they played a role in the grand scheme of my life and one day their overall meaning would be revealed, like a large painting whose outlines and theme have not yet fully emerged. I know now there is no grand scheme, no outlines, no theme, and that the events of my life happen randomly, in a world that is inherently random. But there was something else, I felt a kind of density to my existence that lay somewhere inside me and kept my lucidity in balance, like the little lead weights placed inside rubber figurines to keep them upright. I felt I knew who I was, that I was unique, indispensable. In order to "perform" my life I had learned certain habits and forms of behaviour that gave me the semblance of an ordinary man, just like any other. I knew how to laugh when something funny happened, because at that moment I truly believed it was funny, and my eyes would spontaneously fill with tears when I felt pain or distress. They were faultless displays prompted by fine, clear sentiments that unfolded over the entire day, from the moment I sipped my first café au lait to when I read the evening paper. Every part of myself was securely glued together into a stable and consistent self whose feelings could be named and reveries explained. You might say I was a man who understood the life he lived. A man who thought he could see the purpose and meaning of this life.

And it was this very solid consciousness, which should have fortified me through my illness and boosted my ego, yes, my ego, my strength and my endurance of pain (as invariably happens to all invalids) and transformed me over the course of a few months or years into a model patient, worthy of pity and compassion, that has found itself defeated as all my lucid inner reasoning collapsed, leaving me as I am now, a man with no understanding of anything around him, a little befuddled, a little dizzied by the whirlwind of world events, without any feelings, any pains, any joys.

I'd like to make an observation, in passing, on physical pain and speak on behalf of those that endure such abject, senseless suffering. I will not glorify it as a "noble and admirable" muse without which no great art is possible. I believe a great many more masterpieces were created in a state of calm and plenitude than in the midst of suffering and the gnashing of teeth.

To return to my original point, I'm certain that a single simple event must have caused my illness to muddle all my feelings into an undifferentiated mass and turn my lucidity into a viscid mud that reflects nothing and has no discernible form. I think some event must have caused this to happen, just as something must have caused a fragment of matter to become a stone or a piece of platinum.

Yet it's especially interesting to note the consequences of my inner collapse and confusion of feelings. Sometimes I've been cast as a brave, suffering hero and other times as a lunatic. Neither role particularly suited me, although I am more partial to the latter given I find madness quite appealing as the ultimate attempt to form a new perspective on reality, one completely contrary to the everyday, so that the expression "to be out of one's mind" seems perfectly apt to me, as it implies seeing the world at one remove from rationality.

Copying a drawing through tracing paper is something children like to do, and if the paper moves, the figures come out crooked and distorted. This is the madman's uncanny point of view as he tries to "copy" life while reality shifts a few centime-tres, and he, "out of his mind," recreates it in fantastical forms.

The label of hero I have found much less tenable, but I have never explained my reasons to anyone. It would take too long, and they are far too complicated.

This is what happened: My first experience of horrific pain was after my operation, particularly when my bandages were changed. It was the end of summer and rather than stitch up the wound they left it open to keep it from becoming infected in the extreme heat, thus exposing the very depths of my mus-cles, like a bloodied, beautiful slab of butchered meat. When I gingerly lifted the sheet the nurse covered me with while she was changing my bandages and saw the open wound on my stomach for the first time, I was so struck by its rawness that I could not believe it belonged to my body.

A single instant was not enough to grasp that those flayed, rounded, swollen muscles slick with blood had replaced the smooth, white belly that belonged to me before the operation, as if someone had placed a chunk of butchered meat there to scare me. It gaped like an enormous vagina, its edges bloody and swollen, and the only time I had seen anything like that was when I was out on my carriage and the mare raised its tail for whatever reason to expose a superb scarlet vulva like an exotic flower with thick roselike petals.

But this was my new flesh now, no longer whole, flawless or attractive, now utterly transformed into an unbearably tender wound. This mass of unhealed raw flesh had to be cleaned every day with pure ether to prevent infection. It was barbarically painful. As if dozens of knives were simultane-ously piercing my body, as if dozens of claws were poking around and tearing at all the nerves, as if lava had been poured into my stomach and was advancing towards the brain, the pain virulently spread like fire until the apex of agony had been reached.

To give you a more precise sense of the extent of this pain I should explain that in the first days after the operation these bandages were normally changed under general anaesthetic, and some patients were put under even eight days later because they couldn't stand the agony. My bandages were changed without anaesthetic because chloroform made me agitated and feverish and gave me bad dreams, and also on account of my alleged "heroism," more on which later.

I think the doctor was amazed when I didn't scream or even wince the first time he changed my dressings. After he had fin-ished, he looked at me with surprise.

"I was expecting you to scream the whole sanatorium down . . . I'm truly amazed by your composure, considering we didn't give you any anaesthetic — you're a hero, in your own way . . ."

"Thank you, doctor, but I don't think I deserve your praise, I could easily have screamed."

And I added mentally, "if my experiment hadn't worked." Because it was just a simple experiment I was conducting, using a certain method I will try to explain as precisely as I can, something I had stumbled on to control physical pain during my first days of illness. The whole thing came from a small detail I noticed: while one particular nerve is assailed by pain, the rest of the body, including the brain, continues to function normally. Within this general calm, this hum of activity completely alien to suffering, pain is an invasive nuisance. As it carries out its assault, everything else charges us to stay calm, indifferent, and our thoughts — which are thrown into a nameless chaos as the agony vibrates through the nerves like an electric current — are only waiting for the pain to subside so they can return to their own preoccupations where suffering plays no part except through the vague, yet constant, threat of its return.

While in this state, it's difficult to become absorbed in your usual thoughts because they are fraught with terror and apprehension. It is a well-known fact that in such instances you should try to "distract" yourself and, as far as possible, try to "ignore" the pain by reading the newspaper or engaging in conversation.

Well, I noticed this only made the suffering worse, and I came to the simple conclusion that instead of "ignoring" the pain it had to be given unadulterated "attention." Absolute focus on absolutely every aspect of it. Until you feel it even in the smallest fibres.

So when the pain surged through my ailing limbs, I would put down my book, halt any conversation, and swat away any other thought to observe its dark, abstract journey through a particular part of my body, like a hot stream of water that sprang out of my thigh and split into droplets and rivulets, like a burst of fireworks, then, from time to time, a sharper twinge, as if the rivulets had swelled and the piercing sensation was fanning out through my flesh. It was then that I comprehended the "contours" of the pain and I only had to follow it like a piece of music, with my eyes shut and straining to "listen" carefully to every variation of the tone and intensity of my suffering in the same way I would to the modulations and diversity of a concerto's movement composed of certain refrains and "themes," and just as they would eventually become familiar to me, so did the "composition" of my pain.

Nevertheless, it wasn't enough to keep my suffering in check, so I also violently squeezed the pinkie of my right hand. All the "melody" of my suffering would flow into this finger, like an electric current through a metal tip. And this method could always be counted on as long as I didn't break my concentration on the pain for even one moment by drifting into a reverie, otherwise the agony would again seize control. The pain would stop only if it had my full attention, flooded by lucidity, just as everything we're fully conscious of becomes amorphous and no longer a source of joy or pain. When examined up close, a sensation loses its acuity and colour, just as everything becomes blurred when viewed in a dazzling light.

So when the doctor congratulated me after changing my dressings for the "heroism" with which I endured the pain, instead of offering him any justifications or explanations I should have shown him the pinkie of my right hand. It was always bruised purple after my bandages were changed.

In another instance my "heroism" was even more unexpected. I had adopted an almost cynical, even dissembling pose in order to appear more courageous than I was in reality. But it was nothing more than a state of mind so simple and natural that it's easily explained.

In the previous winter my thigh developed a serious complication that caused a horrible, pus-filled swelling — red, inflamed, extremely painful and raw to the lightest touch. Everyone would walk around my room on eggshells lest any vibration reach my bed and cause me pain, yet I was able to manage the awful agony, even though I took every care to avoid it. A cursory medical examination concluded that the swelling had to be lanced. This had to be done with a needle as thick as a small pipe with no anaesthetic, which would have caused the thigh skin to thicken. After the pus was drained, an antiseptic fluid was syringed in to prevent further infection, and the whole area seemed engulfed in flames. I am describing this in detail in order to explain my subsequent reaction.

The first summer vegetables were ripening at the time, and they gave me terrible stomach cramps and all sorts of unpleasant bowel issues, a particularly disagreeable situation for someone bedridden who is dependent on others for care. What's more, a medical exam revealed that my knees had ossified crookedly and an urgent procedure would be needed to force them back into the correct shape. This procedure took place the following day and it involved stretching my legs with the aid of rubber bands with a sack of sand weighing a few kilograms attached at the end, designed to force my limbs to straighten. It's impossible to describe the pain caused by stretching an ossified joint and forcing it to maintain the exact same position when the muscles around it are completely atrophied. I lay there with my bowels going crazy, the antiseptic burning in my thigh and my leg forcibly extended.

Well, I have to confess, and I hope you'll believe me, that the whole situation made me laugh, or at least smile to myself at the comedy of it. In just a few days my body had developed every possible complication. And I found this hilarious.

In the comedies we see in the cinema, the humour is often derived from the spectacle of a strong, muscular character fighting an agile weakling who can evade the blows, such as, for example, an American policeman and puny Charlot constantly slipping from his grasp. Pitting these two unmatched individuals — one powerful and confident, the other frail and timid — against each other creates the comedy. And this is exactly the situation I found myself in when complications related to my illness started to develop. Every day heralded a new torment, a new form of suffering, another shade of despair, all of them assailing an exhausted body that still, incomprehensibly, found the power to fight, and this unfair fight was the very stuff of comedy. When they extended my leg and the pain started, I wanted to burst out laughing. — "Still there?" I queried the pain.

It was like the stubbornness of the elephant pitted against a mouse. And once it reached that point, the pain started to subside. There is not enough room in a sick body for all the suffering and all the medical complications in the world. In the end, you either have to die or improve enough to remain "sick" for a while longer . . .

And I was granted that privilege.

In the days after the operation, when I started going to the beach again in my carriage, the town looked entirely new and utterly different to the one I had known, transformed by autumn in the same way that some animals shed their skin with the changing of the seasons.

The town wore a new skin, a new sky, a new beach. Each one of its features was filled with an elemental simplicity as if they had only just been sketched and arranged in the landscape, even the walls of the buildings and the asphalt on the roads had been wiped clean of memories. Reality had been reshaped from brand new matter and rebuilt the town in which I now stood, reconfigured, fresh and untried, hollow and weightless, my body a simple outline. The sun was setting on the horizon and the puddles left by the retreating tide reflected back the bruised twilight, transforming it into a dusty antique velvet.

The fishermen returned from their nets with full sacks, and as I wandered through the town I saw all kinds of fish and sea creatures laid out on the slab of a market stall as dark as a train compartment. They were cylindrical and slimy, elastic and meaty, clinging to the ruddy arm of the fishmonger like silver skinned snakes, coiling suggestively around her flesh. The rest of the fish were piled in a basket like heaps of silver and rose gold, and when the woman grabbed a handful their cool mercury brushed against her arm and their dense scales grazed her skin. The basket also held pink shrimps like tender rosebuds, and fish whose bodies seemed like they had been flattened in the belly of a whale, and live lobsters sniffing the air and probing the burly, mustachioed woman with their own whiskers, as if worshipping her beauty. The oysters were enormous fans that had once quivered at the bottom of the sea, in a ballroom illuminated by oceanic phosphorescence and decorated with fantastical algae where drowned beauties from sunken transatlantic ships waltzed in slow circles on the arms of lost sailors ...

There were crabs, with their halo of articulated armoured claws, and as I savoured the salty, vaguely putrid seawater locked inside them I closed my eyes, drunk on that pungent, saline aroma whose broad reach had pulled me to that stall, altered and stinking, like an olfactory trail of sea foam that filled my nostrils with so much delight I thought I would faint.

On some market days the fish stall neighboured a stand of wild flowers and pots of chrysanthemums that replaced the algae as the fish's last adornments, feather-capped chrysanthemums, like powder puffs, with their ruffled petals appearing to be made out of pink silk ribbons or parchment, or torn from an ancient violet ball gown.

And the wives of the Berck fishermen, with their red skirts and thick grey blouses, would sometimes bring to the market the flowers they grew in their gardens along with the fish caught by their husbands, and the fish would be displayed in their stalls next to the chrysanthemums, creating a splendid juxtaposition that painted a fascinating, beautiful picture of their simple lives.

But when I returned to the sanatorium, I was greeted once again by its hushed old suffering, its musty existences, scented with chloroform, shuttered inside gloomy corridors and numbered rooms where the same dramas would blaze up and then fizzle out, like scenes enacted behind a drawn curtain without an audience.

I remember one time when, having returned from an outing in the carriage, I overheard a heated exchange in the room next door between the director of the sanatorium, who was shouting, and a female patient, who was moaning in protest rather than arguing. It was difficult to distinguish exactly what they were saying, but when the director opened the door, the woman's words echoed in the corridor:

"I'll give you my wedding ring . . . I have no use for it now anyway . . ."

"And what am I supposed to do with it?" asked the director. "You should pawn it somewhere."

When the woman was finally alone, lying on the bed, she started moaning to herself again between sighs.

"Ah, you filthy Syrian, you filthy bead merchant, you bandit . . ." and many other curses escaped her mouth, all aimed straight at her husband, whom I had seen visiting her in the sanatorium and who appeared to be Syrian.

This woman had not been seen in the dining hall for several days, and we found out that she was indeed furious with her husband. She had learned from one of the chambermaids that he had left her and was now living in Paris with another woman. He had not paid the hospital bills for almost two months. The sanatorium director clearly considered it out of the question that any patient should get a free ride, and he would have surely mulled over the cold-blooded idea that the woman should receive a special operation that would slice up her intestines and thereby prevent her from taking advantage of free medical care. The idea that an invalid might perpetrate such a swindle seemed so extraordinary and monstrous it tormented his sleepless nights, even though he could blithely snore through a patient's agonising operation, happily oblivious to the screams of pain.

He had known for a few weeks that the Syrian had not paid his wife's bills and was now angry at himself for allowing her to "feast and drink" at their expense. A few days ago he had come to his senses and banned her from the dining hall and only allowed her to take meals in her room. These meals consisted of a cup of sweet tea prepared by the chambermaid and two stale rolls. The patient made no objections to these meals or to any aspect of her situation. She had a few friends in Berck who were willing to smuggle in sausages, biscuits and bananas that she would devour with evident satisfaction. She couldn't move to another establishment since they would require an advance on the fees and inquire about why she had to leave. Besides, in a small place like Berck, news travels fast.

It was impossible for her to stay at the sanatorium and it was impossible for her to leave it. Just one of those desperate situations without a solution. And this patient was likely to remain immobilised in a plaster cast for many years to come. In the end, her sister, a seamstress in Paris, came to her rescue and used her meagre savings along with some borrowed money to pay the bill. The director was good enough to accept the payment and send her on her way without any further unpleasantness. One afternoon when I returned to my room, the sick woman was gone. I had no idea where.

A few days later, I bumped into one of her friends and asked:

"She's gone to her sister's in Paris, they both live in the same room, one of them lying on the bed, the other on her feet all day, both of them mending and sewing for a living."

"How did she get to Paris on a stretcher in a plaster cast?"

"Well, it wasn't easy. They laid her out on the carriage's seats, but she had to get up and walk to get on the train and then get off in Paris, some of the other passengers naturally helped her . . . She could have undone all the progress her treatment had made, but wasn't left with much choice."

But funny, grotesque things also happened in the sanatorium, such as the time a young count from an important aristocratic family checked in for some discreet medical treatment. He was a boy with a shock of blond hair, as yellow as corn, who for some reason had travelled to Buenos Aires where he discovered an extraordinary bounty of prostitutes imported from all over the world, and he devoted all his time to them until his parents summoned him home. He replied that he was having a grand time in Buenos Aires and had no plans to return. They made futile threats and even cut off his allowance, but the young count managed to fund himself by borrowing money from his country's ambassador, who knew his family and had unpaid debts to them. Through some skullduggery, the family ultimately triumphed, and the boy was marched onto a ship under guard to make sure he got home safely.

Unfortunately, their plan failed, because as soon as the ship arrived at Naples the young man scarpered, and after borrowing more money, he took the next boat back to South America, feeling pretty pleased with himself. And this was how after his brief sojourn in Europe the count returned to the city of his dreams, where he stayed for another two years until he fell ill and had to come back.

He made few friends in the sanatorium, and since his treatment consisted mostly of injections, he could still walk, and would often amble into town to frequent an American bar where he had taught one of the waiters how to mix special South American cocktails. He took it as a form of exile, but at least on this desert island he could still get all the drinks he wanted, as well as beautiful girls on occasion, not to mention the latest gramophone records.

The count spent his "Robinson Crusoe" existence amusing himself in this bar, yawning with boredom and getting blind drunk "to while away the hours." On the day before he was due to leave he got so smashed he had to pay a significant penalty to cover the damage he'd done to his room and to wait a few extra days before moving out so that all his clothes could be mended and packed.

But in fact, he hadn't drunk much that evening, it was just that an overwhelming misery had melted his soul, so that when he returned to the sanatorium in the middle of the night, stupefied and confused and showering the hideous, wrinkled night nurse with kisses after she let him in, he opened the door to his room, left it unlocked, and buck naked started to put his things in order. He put his records on the hot radiator, turned on the tap and stuffed his pillow in the sink, carefully placed his mattress in the middle of the floor to stay cool during the night, broke a light bulb and porcelain basin, then, feeling a little sick and anxious not to mess up the room, opened the chest of drawers and threw up all over his clothes.

When the chambermaid entered the next day around lunchtime, she found the count fast asleep in his birthday suit on the mattress on the floor, his mouth partly open, while black molten plastic dripped from the radiator, the records having melted and coated all the pipes in goo.

Stories such as this would travel through the sanatorium and amuse the patients for a few days, to the annoyance of the director, who clearly didn't have a sense of humour.

I spent most of the afternoons away from the sanatorium, taking carriage rides. I so regretted that I couldn't raise myself up from the stretcher and stroke my horse. I felt we were friends, and I would ask someone to feed him the sugar-cube treats I kept for him in the carriage. One time the horse ate so much sugar he got a stomachache and had to rest in the stables for a few days.

Here's how it happened. I was friendly with an elderly lady in the sanatorium and used to chat with her about her son, who was also ill and spent all his time in his room. She was a withered little thing, with a long, thin neck that she would mask by wearing a medallion attached to a black silk ribbon that seemed to tie up her thick veins and prominent Adam's apple like a bundle of vegetables. Everyone in the sanatorium knew she was an absolute miser and had bizarre habits, such as when some hairs fell out she would quickly gather them in her hand and place them back on her head, as if this would stop her from balding. Because she was so afraid of losing her hair, she would never brush it, so that her tangled, dirty, thinning reddish grey locks made her look like a mattress with a few wisps of wool stuffing poking out. Her miserliness was the stuff of rumours that circulated throughout the sanatorium, such as that she drank her tea unsweetened so she could save the sugar cubes in a box. But since she had a certain social standing to uphold, she could never quite bring herself to sell them, out of embarrassment.

One day, as we were talking outside the sanatorium while I was lying in the carriage, I asked her to give my horse a sugar cube. When she saw how the mare greedily devoured the treat, she commented that she hadn't realised horses like sugar.

"And how!" I said. "My mare can't get enough of it."

"Well," she said, "you know, I like your horse and I'm going to bring her some sugar . . . just wait a moment, I'll go and fetch it."

It was the sugar she had pilfered that morning which she now had to find a way to dispose of, particularly as her son had caught wind of her infamous collection and kept scolding her and urging her to get rid of it. So the old lady brought down her box of sugar cubes and the horse had a feast.

I liked to look at my horses' croups, the well-groomed, shiny coats and heavy tails, and when they turned their heads towards me, they seemed to understand how much I loved their large, teary, melancholy eyes and their thick black lips that revealed long, yellowish smoker's teeth. Some young boys, around fifteen years old, also took carriage rides from the sanatorium, and they had somehow come up with a savage form of entertainment that involved pushing the handle of the whip into the mare's vulva until she reared up, maybe from pain, or maybe from pleasure. And the ignorant imps burst into laughter at the animal's antics.

Sometimes they took the horses out for long rides in the countryside, and the animals came back so exhausted, parched and foaming at the mouth the first thing they would do was to gallop to the fountain on the esplanade and gulp down large quantities of water. Being treated this way made them sick, and their owner had only vague suspicions why his horses sometimes got pneumonia and died a few days later. I think this is what must have happened to a young black horse I was very fond of, a muscular, slightly jumpy pony who was my frequent companion on my jaunts. One day when I stayed behind at the sanatorium, a young boy must have taken him out and ran him so ragged he fell ill. When I asked for him to be harnessed to my carriage the following day, the owner told me he wasn't up to it. For a few days I took out a rather docile white mare. And then the dejected owner told me my little horse had died.

"And I sold him," he added. "You can find him at the butcher's."

A few of the butcher's shops in Berck sold only horsemeat. They were all crammed together in the same little street and you could easily distinguish them by the enormous wooden horse heads that hung above their doors. Inside they were impeccably clean, and the deep red carcasses, slightly darker than the ox meat, looked very appetising as they hung against the white, porcelain tiled walls. Sometimes I used to go there and buy a few ounces of "steak tartare," freshly minced horse-meat seasoned with salt and pepper, and eat it just like that without cooking and without bread. The doctors heartily recommended it, and the meat seemed to be perfumed with cold blood and a vague scent of pasture, as if it had been marinated in aromatic herbs.

It was the day before I left for Switzerland that I learned my little horse had died.

I remember that last day in Berck, a cold, cloudy day, a fine, persistent drizzle released a clammy vapour that settled deep inside the lungs, the street's dying lights drowned in a thin veil of fog, and the electric bulbs that illuminated the shopwindows hung eerily like golden fruit shrouded in the smoke of a steamship.

Naturally, not many people had gone out to buy horsemeat that day, and when I entered the butcher's shop in that deserted street I found the owner snoozing on his chair by the counter. He showed me the hanging carcass of my little horse, even gave me a taste of his meat before he sold me a franc's worth of "steak tartare" minced from his flesh, which I ate slowly, savouring his taste with my eyes closed, trying to absorb it deep inside me, so that in this way I could commune with the spirit of the dead animal I loved.

I finished my packing that afternoon and left Berck the next morning, the place where I had lived for three years. The death of my little horse meant the loss of my last dear friend, in a town where I had already lost so many . . .

It would be the last memory I would take from there, the last sorrow.

III

THE TRAIN COMPARTMENT WAS SO STUFFY I OPENED the door to let in some air. I travelled in an old-fashioned carriage with separate compartments having two long benches opposite one another, on one of which lay my stretcher. It was a gloomy winter's day, a fine rain fell on the hills and the cattle in the fields, and I could see the horses and cows closest to the tracks exhaling steamy balls of cotton wool that immediately dissolved in the drizzle.

It was my first train journey in many years. When we stopped at different stations, people would open the door to my carriage and then quickly retreat, explaining to their fellow travellers:

"There's a sick man inside . . . an invalid . . ."

This brought home to me the fact that I was ill, that I was an outsider in the vital, everyday world of the healthy. I wasn't plagued by this sense of separation in Berck, because it was enough to encounter another patient in a carriage, or at meal-times to see all those supine bodies around me to restore my inner equilibrium of calm and indifference that passes for peace in the world of the sick.

As we got closer to Paris, the train passed through suburbs where the grey houses were so close to the tracks that I could see a dirty-nosed child in school uniform eating a sandwich, or women doing the laundry, or an old man contentedly smoking his pipe and watching the train through a window. In one of the streets, I saw a delivery boy on a tricycle laden with parcels, pedalling lazily, a cigarette dangling from the corner of his mouth. Some of the windows were closed, their lacy curtains perhaps concealing only emptiness . . . the train rumbled on . . . and it was those closed windows I would never see again that I found particularly intriguing and exciting . . . the ones I merely glimpsed in passing . . . the window of the compartment rattled as I imagined the gentle, unremarkable daily life playing out behind them . . .

At the station in Paris I had to wait a few hours for the ambulance in a room with enormous windows that gave on to the main hall. I was laid in the middle of the room as if on a catafalque with crowds of people around me like mourners at a funeral, only instead of consoling the family they were offering candy to the corpse, while the deceased himself contentedly puffed on his pipe. The large windows were behind me, but when I caught sight of them in a mirror, I was taken aback. An astonished crowd had gathered on the other side of the glass, pressing their pale noses to it and staring inside, mouths agape. The first row consisted mostly of children, then some taller people immediately behind them, and so on, folks of different heights arranged in tiers, all of them gawping at the "invalid" and whispering, presumably exchanging opinions about the nature, duration and gravity of my illness. In the meanwhile, the commotion in the concourse never paused, trolleys laden with luggage rattled past, shrill whistles pierced the air, a locomotive hissed and the earth trembled as trains passed on the platform underneath us like distant thunder smothered in a subterranean sky.

The ambulance finally arrived and took me to the hotel. I remember that journey through nocturnal Paris, the ambulance windows wide open, like a dizzying trance full of lights and fascinating images flashing past, which I glimpsed with bitter regret knowing that I would leave them behind and forever lose them in that misty rain illuminated by the rosy lights flickering in the streets of the forbidden city. I breathed in the acrid stench of gasoline and decomposing vegetation so characteristic of Paris, and found again the ambiance of the lonely quarters where I used to walk and the joy I felt years ago as I sat on a bench in a side street and gazed at a yellowing banana leaf torn by the wind and floating in a puddle on the pavement, then rested my head on the back of the bench and endlessly murmured to myself, wide-eyed and delirious as a drunk — I'm in Paris . . . in Paris . . . in Paris . . .

So many years of fervent expectation vibrated in this murmur, so many nights when I had lain wide awake, feeding the same reverie — "When I get to Paris . . ." — like an extraordinarily haunting melody keeping sleep at bay and, as I rested in a windowless room, with its locked door and lights playing on the ceiling, my imagination created a secret, private island, a vibrant, lively city all of my own that was surrounded by the musty, muddy darkness of the streets that wound through my provincial town.

And now I possessed all of its reality, I knew its light-filled streets, the shopwindows awash with coloured lights like strange aquariums populated by splendid, pale, slumbering wax mannequins in sumptuous evening dresses with SOLD signs pinned to them along with the price in large red numbers. It was indeed the Paris of my dreams, and it harboured within some of my old provincial sorrows as well as the new ones of lonely, desolate autumn days, the melancholy of street hawkers wheeling carts piled up with bananas and shouting at the top of their lungs, of "musicians" that would stop at a street corner to play the accordion and sing their next hit after distributing sheets of the music and lyrics to their audience gathered in a circle and asking them to attentively follow along:

"It's the third verse, on the back of the page, let's begin!"

And the rasping sigh of the accordion sounded in that sad, gloomy Paris street, accompanied by benevolent voices hoarsely belting out apache songs full of melancholy:

Ce n'est pas une fille des rues, c'est ma régulière ... and other times vaguely obscene:

> *Je l'ai vue nue*
> *plus que nue ...*

It was Paris ... and I was in Paris ... In the evenings, I bought *frites* in the street to warm me up, and as the city came to life I would stop at the entrances of metro stations to watch the exhausted office workers emerge like moles from underground, their faces grave and ashen, as if they had been moulded from grey dough. And I would sit there munching my *frites* and people-watching with the placid, docile wonder of a provincial who has found himself in the greatest city on earth after being plucked out of the back of beyond.

"Eh, do you want to come with me?" a thin, heavily made-up girl would ask, waving a scarf that wafted the cheap scent of snowdrops under my nose.

In my hotel room, with its old, heavy velvet drapes, the rumble of the metro would wake me at dawn and, unable to get back to sleep, I would make coffee using the device I had brought with me, then get dressed and go out into the city.

"You aren't lazy like my other guests," the landlady would tell me. The hotel only had a few rooms so she knew everyone. "When I see you leaving so early in the morning, I wonder if you're taking a trip to Fontainebleau; the only time I go out at this hour is when I'm going there with my daughter and son-in-law."

And because she often forgot my name, she would tell the chambermaid "to make up the room of the gentleman who has just left on a trip" . . .

. . . So the ambulance drove me through those places that seemed like immense warehouses filled with memories and nostalgia, and every car horn, every shout, every light was like a direct, secret signal to the telegraph of my heart, sent from a world that seemed horrifyingly ancient and far away.

My illness made me feel as if I was on the edge of a cluster of events, movements, sounds and lights that constituted the world itself. Later this feeling grew stronger inside me, as I lay in my dark hotel room and could see through the window in the house across the street a brightly lit room with walls full of paintings and two gentlemen, an older one with a beard and moustache, dressed in grey, and a young, thin man with large, dark circled eyes, dressed in black. I could see them so clearly and followed their every movement: They walked around the room and from time to time the older man would take a painting off the wall and explain something enthusiastically, his words accompanied by hand gestures, then hang it back up again. What did the young man say in response? What was depicted in those paintings, who were these men? So many things that I was destined never to find out. There were people and paintings in the world that would remain forever unknown to me, like all the other events that sank into the impalpable substance of the atmosphere, vanishing without a trace and leaving no echo or sign for me to hear. All these things were happening outside of me, people were touching paintings and talking about them, and I had no notion who they were, what the paintings were about, or what was being said about them.

And that thought began to obsess me and make me feel like a stranger in the world, so that for a long while afterwards I would find myself in the middle of a conversation that I thought I was paying attention to or that might have even concerned some grave matter relating to me, and the vision of that room in Paris would suddenly flash before me, immediately followed by the question:

"What are all those paintings I will never see and all those conversations I will never hear?"

My question would magnify every day, with every object I contemplated, until it became a vertiginous part of my subconscious into which I will continue to sink for the rest of my days . . .

I arrived in Switzerland the following evening after leaving Paris at dawn in a train compartment on which the conductor was kind enough to put a RESERVED notice, making me feel like an important politician. He did all he could for me, and when the train stopped at stations he would rush in with sandwiches and bananas which he thrust on me with all the timidity and awkwardness of his youth. When we came to the border and his shift was over, he popped in to my compartment to wish me "bon voyage," and then, after a brief hesitation, blushing all the way to his ears, said:

"And good health to you, my child," though he was roughly the same age as me.

When I disembarked at the station where I was supposed to take the funicular, everything was covered in snow. A special compartment was attached to the funicular for me, large enough for my stretcher to fit inside. Clearly it was normally used to transport corpses, and one must have been in it quite recently because I could see on one of the seats some leaves that had probably fallen off a bouquet of flowers and on the floor some pine branches and drops of wax that suggested the presence of mourners holding candles.

Before beginning our ascent, my compartment passed through a wasteland of derelict warehouses, the dancing snowflakes falling on crates and barrels illuminated by anaemic electric lights, creating the impression that I was travelling to the end of the world. These desolate spaces reminded me of winter walks through my hometown, when I would wander by the railway tracks past warehouses just like these, and the familiar decay broke my heart. It was the very same silence, the same solitude, the same snowflakes that danced in the pale illumination of the very same electric lights.

They shuttered me in for the ascent and I saw nothing more, then when we reached the top I was transferred to an ambulance that took me to Leysin. But when we reached the sanatorium and I was carried outside, I suddenly saw the immense valley below the mountain, aglow with thousands of lights sparkling in the darkness, an earthly sky crammed with constellations, mirroring the heavens. The constellations of villages at the bottom of the valley were like the twinkling, glittering lights on a Christmas tree bedecked with cheap ornaments. I breathed in deeply and felt weightless, the air seemed clear and pure, knife cold, clean as crystal, and my lungs effortlessly absorbed this new atmosphere that surrounded me as if it were silkier, finer and lighter than any I had ever encountered.

"I have been reborn," I exclaimed enthusiastically.

And when the nurse came to wash me, change my clothes

and tuck me into the freshly made bed vaguely scented with camphor, it was as if I had truly entered a new world, thoroughly clean and scrupulously disinfected. That scent seemed like an extension of the sanatorium and its perfect cleanliness.

In the morning, after scrubbing me down with cold water, they opened the doors wide and rolled my bed onto the terrace, and I saw the Rhine valley opening out in front of my eyes, the river sparkling in the sunshine and flowing like mercury through the mountains. At the bottom of the valley there were villages and houses, cattle and people, all of which I could see through the clear air and even manage to follow their activity. At the edge of the valley a waterfall surged in silver streams, and further down I could see a bridge tiny as a hairpin that minuscule trains passed over like earthworms into the belly of the mountain.

In Leysin, the village below my clinic, I could see the rows of sun terraces belonging to other sanatoriums where the orthopaedic patients sunbathed in the nude, while those with pulmonary conditions took the air on the terraces of their rooms, sheltered by curtains, a configuration that from a distance looked like a beehive.

Alpine wisteria glistened with drops of melted snow, and in the pine forest surrounding the clinic wisps of white mist clung to the trees. But it wasn't cold, and the nude patients lay sweating in the heat of the sun, their heads covered by wide-brimmed straw hats. Almost all of them were tanned.

"What time is it, please?" I asked the nurse.

A patient who was surveying the valley through a brass telescope answered "10:30," without consulting his watch. He was an Englishman with whom I would later become acquainted. The telescope was so powerful he could see the clock on the school building in the village, and that's how he could tell me the exact time.

It was a fantastic telescope and I would later make use of it, too, for my own purposes. Inside it was engraved with a floral motif and the name *Constant Demoisin, Opticien du Roy,* as well as a date, which might have been 1753. After I handled it, I detected its sharp scent on my fingers, a bit like mouldy cheese, reminding me of when I was a child and I used to rummage in drawers and fiddle with whatever brass objects I found there, such as broken door handles or curtain rings, which I pilfered to use as props in a magic trick I had learned from some manual I'd stumbled upon . . . And I paused with the telescope in my hand, years away from the valley and the sun that blazed above it.

As I lay on the terrace, my white bedclothes reflecting back the rays of the sun, I could see the main village street at the bottom of the valley and even distinguish some minuscule bodies walking on the cobbled path. Directly in front of the sanatorium, in the valley below, lay a drainage ditch with a huge boulder on top of it that captivated me for some reason. It was like a period at the end of a sentence. My eyes would scan the valley, the street, the pine forest, then would rest on the boulder, the full stop, and then I would start again from the beginning. Even after reading my book, I would put it down and look again at that large rock and it seemed to say "full stop." A "full stop" to my reading that day, and, with time, a "full stop" to every other act in my life.

Some days the boulder took on a momentous significance, such as when the doctor came to conduct his weekly examinations. I would promise myself that once I was cured I would walk all the way to that rock and sit on it for a few seconds to fully comprehend that I could walk and that it's in my power to touch the boulder I'd been staring at in despair from a distance for so many days. "When will that day come?" I would ask myself, desperately expecting an answer from the rock, "When will my legs function again so that I can walk there and touch it?" And in this way it became a symbol of healing for me, a palpable sign that I was well again, and if anyone were to ask me what would be the first thing I do the day I realise I could walk again, if I would go home or maybe return to Paris, I would answer quickly and without any hesitation: "I will walk to that boulder and touch it."

Anyway, although my treatment was unchanged and I thought I would be bedridden for a long time, possibly without a plaster cast, to my immense surprise the doctor told me I could start walking again, slowly at first since I still had an open wound, and so I was able to touch the boulder much sooner than I had imagined.

Over the coming days I managed to walk to the rock, but the effort completely exhausted me, because though it didn't seem too far away when seen from my bed, it took much longer than I expected given that the road wound behind houses hidden within the folds of the valley. By the time I finally touched it I could barely breathe, and when I looked up at my sanatorium and its terrace it was with an expression of intense fatigue rather than pride.

I thought it must have been my exhaustion that stopped me from experiencing anything special on the day I touched the rock, despite the fact that I had fervently dreamed of that moment for so long. But the same thing happened in the following days — the air around me was hot and dry, everything plain and ordinary, walking no longer felt like a novelty, and I couldn't summon up the exhilaration I had imagined. All my intense desire had drained away like the charge from a dying battery, my inner world as ashen as the pavement I walked on and just as dull, bereft of resonance. It was just another confirmation of my belief that I should harbour no expectations. All of reality was at my disposal if I could be content simply to inhale it, then immediately exhale it again in one specific moment, without any plans or illusions.

Besides, when I started walking again I found new diversions. In my sanatorium, I was surrounded by the old and infirm. It was isolated from the village, high up on a road where few people ever passed. The road itself was beautiful and led nowhere in particular, winding through the mountains towards fields covered with alpine flowers and ancient pine forests. Sometimes I would see lovers strolling there.

When I left Berck, I imagined I was going to a sanatorium full of patients animated by cheerfulness and youth, but I had ended up in a desolate place, a dull, depressing villa where old ladies knitted all day with their eyeglasses perched on the end of their noses and several congested Englishmen played bridge in their rooms with gravity and intense concentration.

As soon as I started walking again and took my first steps in the sanatorium, the dreams and illusions I had conjured up during my years of confinement became tainted by a caustic virulence accompanied by extremely naive delusions:

"So, now that I can finally walk, I'll be able to strike up a conversation with beautiful women as they promenade in the evenings . . ."

And I dreamt of splendid chambers where beautiful patients with rouged cheeks and attired in peignoirs barely concealing their nudity invited me to spend the siesta hours in their company, and every afternoon I would be a guest in a new room where I would meet and fall in love with fascinating naked countesses adorned with pearl necklaces and magnificent bracelets, because I had a special predilection for countesses in my dreams.

I was burning with anticipation for the moment when I would find myself in such a refined sanatorium where those open arms would ardently embrace me.

The day when I could go out with my friends finally came. They were two Englishmen, one on crutches, almost fully cured, who had worked as a forestry inspector in Scotland, the other one, who suffered from kidney disease, had been an engineer in Auckland, New Zealand, where he had been a partner in a construction company. Every week, this former engineer received enormous parcels full of newspapers and magazines illustrated with splendid photographs of the New Zealand countryside, with silver waterfalls in forest clearings, and one was of an elderly native sitting beside the water, his curly grey hair mirroring the cascade. I didn't think that such indigenous people still existed, braving the river in dugouts, with magical amulets around their necks.

I mentioned this to the engineer as I looked at a photograph of some fetishes artfully carved in jade. He laughed and produced from the pocket where he kept his keys the very same amulet from the photograph. I was so astounded to see it in real life at the very moment it was for me still part of the fragile and tenuous realm of the printed image, that the engineer had to place it in my hand so I could touch it, hold it, and, especially, lift it up to the light to examine the extraordinary waves and shadows shifting through the petrified waters of the translucent jade.

It was unimaginably beautiful, a tiny sculpture of an animal with enormous eyes and an open mouth through which the engineer had attached his key ring. When tapped, it made a dull, dry sound but with a short, crystalline echo, a tiny noise I'd never heard before. Surely there must be thousands of such noises in the world that are lost to us, clinks, sounds and notes and also certain hues within the translucence of water, glass, or precious stones, all of which escape our notice. I kept the jade amulet in my room next to my bed for a few days and sometimes when I woke up at night I would bring it close to my eye, and every second I discovered new phantasmagorical images inside its translucent kaleidoscope.

It was in the company of the engineer and forestry inspector that I ventured for the first time on the mountain road that passed in front of the clinic and where patients with pulmonary disease were often seen on walks, picking flowers and taking the fresh alpine air.

As we rested on a stone bench, I heard my English friends whispering to each other:

"Do you think she'll come today?"

"Maybe she's already gone . . ."

"It's too early . . . if she's coming at all, it will be around this time . . ."

"Alright, we'll wait, we haven't got anything better to do."

And they both broke into laughter, which left them rather breathless, then exchanged sly looks, as if they were thinking of some secret, perverse vice they shared.

It was indeed a vice, but an innocent one, a mild flirtation with a girl they would see picking flowers every day, to whom they'd never spoken but only smiled at and, in the past few days, greeted with a slight nod. For this smile and small token of sympathy they would venture out every day as early as possible and install themselves on the bench, whispering and giggling with an immense childish satisfaction.

When I asked them what they were talking about, they refused to tell me at first, but when a nurse informed me about their "idyll," they confessed everything and pointed her out to me one afternoon. She was a Swiss girl with a long equine face, and her grey eyes betrayed something wild, yet timid. Her ashen complexion and the purple blotches on her face left no doubt that she suffered from pulmonary disease. She wore a beret and a short blue coat with brass buttons onto which she had pinned a badge with white and red lines, the emblem of a friendship and temperance society. The image of an eagle topped the badge, and I recall someone from the sanatorium remarking that this symbol had been a rather poor choice because eagles weren't abstinent.

She was wearing boots made of soft deerskin, and I remember thinking it was the perfect footwear for a walk in the mountains during early spring. Now the three of us would all smile and nod at her discreetly, and she seemed to be touched by this, but a few days later when we passed her on the road as she was walking down the mountain I let my companions walk on ahead and I spoke to her spontaneously, without embarrassment:

"Excuse me for a moment, there is something I would like to tell you."

She stopped and blushed profusely, fiddling with the blue flowers in her hands.

"So, my friends would very much like to make your acquaintance, but they haven't been able to find anyone who might introduce you to them. And because I thought you'd understand their situation and wouldn't be offended, I plucked up the courage to talk to you, so I hope you don't mind or think me rude."

While I was talking, one of my friends heard my voice and turned around to find me conversing with the mysterious girl. As if he'd just had the biggest shock of his life, his expression changed into one of utter stupefaction and wonder, like something truly extraordinary had happened. Extending an arm, he pointed at me and started to mumble unconsciously:

"Look, he's talking to her ... look ... he's talking to her ... ."

When I motioned them over, they seemed completely overwhelmed and, even though these friends of mine were men of a considerable age, they blushed like schoolboys when they shook the girl's hand. It was as if I had performed a feat of daring they never thought possible.

In this way, they finally managed to animate their "idyll" and graduate, after months, from smiles and discreet, friendly nods to conversation with "the girl who gathers flowers," who even accepted an invitation to afternoon tea.

At that point, my interest in this mysterious girl started to wane, but something much more dramatic happened on that isolated mountain road, much more embarrassing and rather shameful. And even today, when I recall what I did, it gnaws at me, even though I've experienced so many embarrassing situations since then that it's been somewhat dulled by oblivion, not least because I no longer judge myself too harshly for my moral failings.

But since I am not writing this book either for my own spiritual solace or for the reader's, I will relate this event, which was as horrible and mortifying for me as it was for everyone else involved.

When, on my crutches, I would go for walks to the stone bench outside the clinic, I would meet some pensioners from a magnificent sanatorium nearby, a huge establishment with extraordinarily comfortable, luxurious rooms, and naturally very expensive. I reasoned that these pensioners must have been quite rich, but I wasn't particularly interested in them and had no desire to know them. They all seemed to be gravely ill, prematurely aged, their faces pictures of anguish and anxiety, their minds full of worries about their temperature and congested lungs. They were the "sombre" pensioners, but I knew the sanatorium was also inhabited by cheerful young people, splendid women and handsome men who spent their nights and afternoons revelling clandestinely in defiance of their illnesses, and these were the ones I wanted to meet.

Going to the village to meet them was out of the question until I was stronger on my feet, until I was capable of walking and standing up for a few hours. Though that fabled sanatorium was close by, I didn't know anyone there who could introduce me to the people I was interested in meeting. This was why I struck up a conversation with the "sombre" pensioners, in the hope that they would be the conduit to the "frivolous" youth inside.

The pensioners were accompanied by a young girl of around eighteen, with a completely nondescript, freckled face and a slight stoop, who wore the same grey coat and green scarf around her neck every day and would occasionally cough into her handkerchief or stop at a bench to catch her breath.

I decided to talk to her even though we hadn't been introduced, just like I had done before, then flirt with her so we would be on friendly terms and get into the habit of visiting one another to borrow books and newspapers, until it would naturally occur to her to introduce me to the others in the sanatorium.

My plan was to catch her when no-one else was walking down the road or when she had stopped for a break, and then make my move. I tried to catch her eye a few times, and although she must have noticed, she didn't given me any sign of encouragement. She would walk on with a cold, indifferent expression, staring straight ahead, her manner as unexpressive as her freckled cheek.

"Surely she would be flattered that I'm flirting with her," I told myself. "She's not really much of a looker, so I can't imagine she gets a lot of attention in the sanatorium."

And one day, at an opportune moment, I decided that I would go and talk to her. I was a few steps ahead and waited for her to catch up. Feeling very sure of myself, I drew closer to her, took off my hat and pretty much repeated, I believe, the speech I'd made to the Swiss girl wearing the temperance badge:

"Excuse me, Miss, there is something I need to talk to you about and I'd like to introduce myself . . ."

I think this is as far as I got, because while I was talking she walked straight past, merely throwing me an accusatory glance as she continued on her way, stiff and proud as if no-one had spoken to her, leaving me behind hat in hand, balancing on my crutches and babbling to myself the rest of the speech I had prepared.

I was absolutely enraged. In a single instant, all of my previous suppositions had been reversed, like a pendulum that having swung in one direction was now swinging back to the opposite side. That evening, I told my friends the whole story.

"Don't waste your time conversing with an ugly girl," I said to them, "she won't be used to the attention so she'll think you're out to seduce her. This one will likely start spreading a story in her sanatorium that she was assaulted in the woods by a lecher who wanted to have his way with her . . . ha! ha! . . ."

But the most embarrassing part of it, which I recall with utmost shame, happened the following day while I was on my usual walk with my friends. As she passed us, I murmured viciously to them, loud enough for her to hear:

"Well, I have no regrets . . . she *is* pretty ugly."

I think she must have heard me because she started coughing, probably out of indignation. My swift revenge satisfied me. I looked forward to telling her, once I got to know her at the sanatorium, that I was no lecher and certainly had no intention of forcing myself on her. In fact, only a few days later I met one of the young men from her sanatorium. I was sure that one day she and I would cross paths again. Soon enough, I was a regular visitor to the sanatorium for the rich, and in the corridors I would see beautiful women and elegant young men, although I would get to know them only later.

The day when I was introduced to my "ugly girl" finally came. It was a dry, grey afternoon, balmy and overcast, and my friend and I had just accompanied one of the female patients to the funicular and were saying goodbye to her on the platform. All of her friends were gathered there, the sanatorium so distinguished as to have its own funicular station.

I spotted the "ugly girl" at the edge of the group that had come to see off the woman on the platform. She saw me too and appeared to blush slightly. I asked my friend if he could introduce me. While I was talking to him, I could see her watching us and guessed that she had worked out what was going on.

"Why do you want me to introduce you to her?" my friend asked. "There's no point . . . the girl is a mute . . ."

"What are you talking about?" I asked him, astounded.

"I'm telling you, she's a mute . . . I mean, she can't talk, she has an extremely severe form of laryngitis and isn't allowed to eat solids or speak . . . besides, even if she tried, she could only let out an incomprehensible growl because her vocal chords are so ravaged by tuberculosis . . . the doctors say she won't last much longer . . ."

At that moment the funicular arrived and everyone was fussing over the patient who was about to depart. Before leaving the station, I looked into the "ugly girl's" eyes and felt the full weight of her reproach. I drifted away overcome with bitterness and despair, while a voice inside me kept repeating like a broken record, "she's mute . . . she's mute . . . she's mute . . ."

Reading these words again, I am filled with wonder as I discover the exact reflection of everything that has happened in reality. It's so hard to disentangle it from all the things that never happened! So hard to purge this reality from the slag of dreams and interpretations that have deformed it. At every moment my mind is filled with alternative images, different reveries, or simple, seductively luminous visions that I must swat aside in order to retain the logic of my narrative, constantly astounded that I'm able to write something that makes any sense at all. But sometimes I'd also like to record all my daydreams and nocturnal dreams in order to create a true image of the illuminated burrow that lies sunken in my most familiar, intimate darkness.

Maybe one day I will be able to write down all the adventures I've had in my dreams, which are just as vivid as real life, or maybe my strength will wane and I won't be able to write anything at all . . . And this would sadden me, because I would like to leave a record of the intense, passionate dreams that have amused and fascinated me more than my waking hours.

Right now, for example, I recall a tiny, isolated fragment from a dream and immediately sense it could grow into something vaster, I imagine all the adventures the characters conjured by my unconscious mind could have inside its world. But for now, I can only grasp the beginning of these sagas, which promise to be so entertaining . . .

. . . Something was happening in town, a kind of change that I can only describe as a form of "specialisation." The streets themselves were the same, but all the shops and institutions began to reflect their "purpose": the train station was polished black like a gigantic locomotive whose entrance was a fire door and whose platform faced the boiler; the post office resembled a postbox painted in yellow with blue stripes; one of the bookshops was shaped like an inkwell and another like a beautifully bound novel; all the coffee shops had transformed into cream cakes; the gramophone stores were huge funnels; and the butcher's shop looked like a ham shank . . . Yet all of this only made a vague impression on me and completely disappeared from my thoughts when I entered the butcher's shop to pick up a few things for my evening meal. The true surprises and marvels were waiting for me inside. It was a shop with shelves and counters, just like any other, but the walls were an impressive mosaic made of sausage meat, the shelves were thin slices of cured fatback fortified by a special process that made them gleam like ivory, and the counters were carved from pâté in aspic, hard as glass and sparkling clean like every counter in any decent butcher's shop.

Feasting your eyes on these marvels couldn't help but give you a deep sensory delight, but two curious details particularly intrigued me: firstly, the owner, a jolly man with a moustache, was dressed like a sexton, and secondly, the package he handed me bore the label: MADE BY RADIO.

What did the sexton outfit and the message on my cold meats signify? I was dying to find out, so as I was paying I questioned the owner, who was alone in the shop at that early hour.

"During the day I wear the normal white apron that you'd expect to see on a butcher," he said, "but you've come before I had the chance to change out of my uniform, which I had to wear because I was delivering some wreaths to a big house . . ."

Noticing that I was even more confused, he elaborated:

"When I first married, I was a funeral director with a beautiful parlour, stocked to the hilt with coffins, wreaths, lamps and all other funeral paraphernalia, it really was a pretty good situation, and pretty profitable too. I kept it going for a few years with my wife's help, until my father-in-law died and left this butcher's shop to his only daughter in his will. It was much more lucrative than the funeral business, because people eat ham and sausages every day, but don't die every day. Still, I didn't want to give up my trade completely, because it was profitable enough, so I decided to divide my time between coffins and cold cuts. And because the rent on my funeral parlour had skyrocketed, I thought I might as well run both businesses from here. All the housewives in the neighbourhood know that on Tuesdays, Thursdays and Saturdays they can come here and purchase the freshest meats at good prices, and on Mondays, Wednesdays, and Fridays (when the zealots of the town are fasting and not eating meat anyway) we offer funeral services.

"Anyway, to spare my customers from having to buy foie gras in a store where coffins and wreaths are stacked side by side with salami and pastrami, and because, as you can see, each building in our town is specially designed to illustrate its purpose and each store reflects the products it sells, on days like today, when this is a butcher's shop, its exterior resembles an enormous shank of ham and its interior walls are made of sausage meat, the shelves are cured lard, the counters are finished in aspic, while on the days when it becomes a funeral parlour, I can transform it in fifteen minutes (with the help of a few accessories and a specially made mechanism involving hooks and screws) into a skull with yellow teeth and gaping eye sockets. Everything remains in its place, all I have to do is cover the walls with black cloth, wrap up the sausages and hams in dark silk and decorate them with silver candlesticks like you might see at a wedding, only that my candles are black, and if you were to scratch them you would notice they are made of minced pork.

"These black and silver decorations completely transform the shop into something funereal, tenebrous . . . black and silver . . ."

He fell into a deep reverie, then, after a few moments, whispered to me sagely:

"It's all about the colour scheme, you could paint the most delightful, splendid rose garden in black and silver and it would look funereal . . . black roses with silver leaves . . . deathly . . . sinister . . . we are programmed to respond to those colours in a certain way, to perceive them as symbols, it is a deeply ingrained instinct."

He lowered his voice and a smile stretched beneath his moustache as he added, confidentially:

"I challenge you to do an experiment. Go home and decorate . . . hmm . . . the lavatory . . . hmm! You understand . . . hmm! The loo, if you will . . . well, then, go home and cover its walls with black paper and hang up some wreaths and banners inscribed with ETERNAL REMEMBRANCE and WE WILL REMEMBER YOU FOREVER . . . well, I can guarantee that . . . hmm! . . . it will no longer be fit for its purpose . . . your entire household will become constipated in a matter of days, of that I can assure you!"

I impatiently waved my hand and he took the hint that it was time to stop.

But I still had to solve the mystery of the inscription on my packet of charcuterie, MADE BY RADIO. When I asked him to explain, the butcher-cum-undertaker seemed surprised by my confusion.

"Have you really not heard of this invention?"

I had to confess that I had no idea what he was talking about.

"I believe you . . . only I can't imagine that anyone in this day and age hasn't heard of a 'Manufacturing Radio' . . . even a child could tell you what it is . . . Have you heard of bicycles? . . ."

"Please drop the sarcasm and just explain it to me, if you don't mind . . ."

"With pleasure . . . with pleasure . . . please follow me . . . to the manufacturing room."

He took me next door to a room where I could see an extraordinary machine that resembled a radio, only three times larger and with a large opening where the speaker should be. Inside the opening was a chamber with white, gleaming walls.

"What frequency do you want to tune in to?" asked the undertaker/pork butcher.

"I don't care . . ."

"In that case, we'll tune into one at random . . ."

He turned a knob, and as we waited for the tubes to warm up I noticed a list stuck on the front of the device just like you would see on a normal radio, only instead of cities with their broadcasting stations, it was an inventory of various European factories, underneath each one in smaller letters the names of the products manufactured there, including some famous brands I recognised. When the tubes lit up, the butcher turned the knob again and the dial stopped at SARDINES A L'HUILE Portugalia, and after a brief whirr, a handsome, appetising tin of sardines gradually began to materialise inside the white chamber, as if crystallising out of condensed air, slowly assuming form.

"Please try the sardines, they are the best on the market . . ."

And to my astonishment, he put the tin in my hand and I noticed it had the same peculiar label as my packet of charcuterie.

"I still don't understand . . ." I mumbled.

"I will explain everything," said the butcher. "You are clearly not familiar with this machine. It was invented around ten years ago. It's called a Manufacturing Radio and, just like any other invention, it's based on a fairly simple principle. I assume you're familiar with the way a conventional radio operates? Musical waves float inside a silent room and the radio can untangle this melodic essence from the amorphous air, cleanse it of smoke, microbes and all other useless elements and deliver it as music, purged of all impurities, to the listener's ear. The machine in front of you works in the same way. Behind it, hidden from view, is a box I fill every day with ground meat, fish, various scraps of fabric I find around the house, ribbons, old bits of iron, flour, wine, paper, orange peel, matchboxes and used stamps, anything I can find, absolutely everything . . . and in much the same way that a radio creates music, this machine can create a tin of sardines if I set the dial to the 'manufacturing' frequency and tune into a sardine factory. Then it selects all the materials it needs from the hodgepodge in the box and creates the desired product, in the same way that a standard radio would pluck out the correct musical notes from the impure air and construct a Beethoven symphony . . . it's simple, really . . .

"And, as you can see from this list, the machine can tune into the 'manufacturing frequencies' of a wide range of factories and create any object you desire . . . I know you're wondering why every household doesn't buy this machine and create everything they want, so there would be no need to ever visit a shop again . . . When these devices first hit the market folks were in an uproar, there were protests, strikes, until the state intervened and introduced strict regulations that they can only be used by those with a licence to sell the goods that are produced in this way with the profits taxed at a high rate.

"At the same time, factories continue to manufacture as usual because some customers still prefer the real thing. They say the radio produced food has a bland, artificial taste, in the same way that some music aficionados refuse to listen to a concert on the radio because to them it is so altered they cannot consider it real music . . .

"So hopefully now you understand why I have to add that label to what I sell. I only have a licence to create charcuterie products, but I made that tin of sardines just to demonstrate what the machine is capable of . . . It can make anything you want . . ."

While he was talking, he turned the knob again and a splendid, pure silk tie slowly began to materialise in the machine's special chamber. After that, he also created for me a packet of foreign cigarettes, a watch, and a thick woolen scarf.

"What do you say to a bottle of French champagne?"

Needless to say, I had never seen anything like it in my life.

The butcher carefully set the dial to the frequency of one of the most renowned champagne cellars. When the bottle was ready, he took it out but cursed loudly when he realised it was uncorked and full of cufflinks.

"What's the matter?" I asked, confused.

"There must have been some interference . . . just like with normal radios, sometimes you get two separate stations playing at the same time, and when that happens you end up with an item that is a mixture of two products. One time it created dinner plates made out of blotting paper, another time it was a fox fur made out of cherry leaf tea. And then there was the time it produced a perfect, yet useless typewriter. It was made of cheese."

I thanked him for his illuminating explanations and made for the door.

"At the moment," he added, "the Japanese stations are flooding the market, if you tune into Tokyo you can have as many electric bulbs and bicycles as you want. It takes about half an hour for a European station to materialise a bicycle, and I need to fill the box at the back twice to provide all the materials required, but a Tokyo station can create one in ten minutes and only uses one full box."

Suddenly I remembered that I needed to clarify something in order to test the radio analogy.

"And parasites . . . is the device ever prone to parasites?"

"Well of course, absolutely," laughed the butcher. "For instance, when I want to make sausages and the device falls prey to parasitic oscillation, something else comes out, exactly in the same shape . . ." He whispered in my ear: "Excrement . . . excrement, pure and simple . . ."

And with those words my visit to the butcher's shop concluded. I thanked him again and left.

Three of my friends were waiting for me in the street, but they had also taken on an extraordinary appearance. One of them was blue, his skin enamelled head to toe like the dishes and basin in a kitchen, because in the land of "specialisation" people took on the appearance of their profession, and my friend was an engineer in an enamelware factory, while another friend wore cellophane clothes and his body had the dark transparency of a radiograph.

"You know, I've always been a sickly man," he explained when I asked him about his appearance. "I'm always getting X-rayed to find out what's wrong with me, so I finally decided to transform myself into one and wear cellophane clothes so that at any moment I can see what's going on in my body."

The third one had the most amazing green eyes but no other distinguishing features, only when he offered us candy did I realise they were watches that melted in your mouth.

"I think you are five minutes fast," observed my blue friend, in the same tone that he might have used to remark that the bonbon was rather sour.

This third man was an artist renowned for his fantastical creations, and when he put the candy in his mouth I noticed it had porcelain dolls for teeth and his tongue was split into thin, red ribbons, like moist, fleshy chrysanthemum petals. And when I looked at his eyes more closely, I saw they were green shards from a soda bottle.

With this last astounding detail, my dream came to an end.

IV

DURING BEAUTIFUL WINTER DAYS THE CLOUDS sometimes stretched over the Leysin valley like a vast, sumptuous
carpet of white cotton wool tinged with pink, while the sky
was astonishingly clear and blue like seltzer bottles. Patients
sunbathed nude on the terrace of the sanatorium even though
all the roofs around them glistened with snow undisturbed in
the pure, still air of the valley.

It was carnival season and the patients had decided to
organise a masked ball and other entertainments in the sanatorium's lounge. Everyone was to be in mask and costume, even
those who needed to be brought in on stretchers by the nurses
and porters. The preparations had gone on for days and everyone was buzzing with excitement by the time the eve of the
party arrived. It was one of those mild, serene winter days, and
all the patients who could still walk were running around the
terrace in the buff, cracking jokes and discussing the next day's
event.

Even the nurses took part in the party preparations and

no-one gave much thought to their treatment, and when the doctor arrived for his usual rounds he was greeted with such applause and cheers he couldn't get a word in edgeways. But no-one really minded, because they felt the patients should be allowed to have some fun once in a while.

I had a harlequin costume with black and yellow diamonds made for me, and even though I was still on crutches, it didn't matter, I was a handicapped harlequin. In the evening, we all went downstairs and admired each other's costumes. There was a pale, thin young lady who suffered from a pulmonary illness and who had come dressed as a marquise, with a bright white woolen wig, red heeled shoes, a violet silk dress, and some black beauty marks stuck on her face and décolletage, creating the image of a frail aristocrat, her fragile chest almost skeletal. She was accompanied by her brother, a robust, athletic young man who had driven his motorcycle all the way from France with nothing else but the clothes he was wearing, a tunic and khaki trousers with leather gaiters. For a costume, he wrapped his head in a scarf and said he was an Arab.

There was also a young man who'd had a knee operation and came dressed as a baron, another was a heavily powdered Pierrot, another a Turk in shalwars clinched by a belt, a fez atop his head. Not many women were present, and apart from the nurses, who were not in costume because they were still on duty, and the bedridden patients could call them at any time, there was only the marquise, a young girl dressed like a Tahitian in a grass skirt, wreathed in leis, and two old ladies who had brought their knitting along. Among some of the patients who were lying prone and not in costume were my English friends, who had decided that wouldn't bother getting dressed up because they were planning on getting drunk, as well as three other patients: one from another sanatorium, an elderly, jolly Frenchman whose hair was completely white, and a very young Swiss boy, around fourteen years old, who became tipsy after his first glass of wine.

It took a while for the party to warm up and an awkward atmosphere lingered in the room for some time, only long faces everywhere, because the patients didn't really know each other that well. It was up to the nurses to make the introductions. But once the radio was turned on, the air became inebriated with jazz and the first bottles of wine were uncorked. In a break, someone turned off the music and the marquise sat down at the piano and started playing a tune, at first with one finger, then with both hands, and began to sing a funny chansonette while we joined in the chorus. The piano, untuned, sounded more like a tambourine, and it wobbled a little on the parquet floor, causing a wooden screen and a bronze candelabrum on a small table to vibrate, as if the flowers painted on the faded screen and the ancient candelabrum had come alive and started partying with us, bouncing along to the rhythm of the hands falling on the keys as if it were a dance tune. The young motorcyclist also had his turn on the piano, and he played pretty well.

The wine was flowing freely, plenty for everyone. Then the patients started ordering more, demanding it be put on their bill. Everyone was a little giddy, the Englishmen had ordered brandy and soda while the Frenchman was treating everyone to champagne. As the young motorcyclist was playing, the candelabrum and flowers on the screen danced even more wildly, vibrating more intensely, while the piano strings endured such a pounding it seemed they might snap any moment. It was really quite a ridiculous scene, especially when the young man sang along with his sister, the marquise, who had torn off her wig and looked even more frail and sickly in her stylish dress:

> *Mon vieux, tu as bonne mine . . .*
> *T'as dû changer de cuisine . . .*

It was almost two a.m., from time to time a buzz from the corridor would beckon one of the nurses, then we heard the quiet drone of a car outside, the doctor's car. So, something serious must have happened. I cornered one of the nurses and asked what was going on.

"It's Miss Corinde, you know, the young nun with TB peritonitis. The doctor is here to attend to her . . . I think he's brought some oxygen with him."

Just at that moment, the "marquise" tugged on my sleeve, signalling me to follow her. I was the only one still sober enough to stand.

"Where are we going?" I asked her in the corridor.

"Please come with me to see Corinde . . . she's in agony, and I want to see her one last time . . ."

"In this ridiculous costume?"

"So what? You think she has any idea what's going on around her?"

A heavy silence hung in the corridor, a feeble lamp cast its sinister light outside the dying woman's room, faint echoes reached us from the lounge.

Mon vieux, tu as bonne mine . . .
T'as dû changer de cuisine . . .

We waited for a nurse to leave the room so as not to disturb the patient by opening the door, then the "marquise" and I went in.

So many people were crowded round the bed we couldn't see anything: the patient's mother, a small, wrinkled woman with dirty grey hair in a bun, two nurses, and the doctor holding the oxygen tank. My companion drew closer, then stepped back.

"She's so beautiful . . . have a look . . . ," she said.

When one of the nurses moved away I took a step towards the bed and looked at the sick girl. Was she really the sick nun everyone at the sanatorium whispered about? I had encountered many nuns before, all of them old or ugly, who appeared aged before their time, tormented by secret maladies. And now this nun, with her delicate profile and pink nose, fever blooming in her cheeks like some kind of expertly applied makeup, her half-closed, almond green eyes, so splendid, her hair so black it glistened with a blue halo around her head as it spread like waves on the pillow. What was the point of this beauty? Could such beautiful nuns really exist? Surely they were only found in the books I used to read as a child, books I would buy for 5 bani, with titles such as *The Beautiful Nun*. My entire childhood suddenly gained a deeper resonance, like a bell at the bottom of a lake.

And me, standing in my harlequin costume in front of her? Were all the romantic situations, all the extraordinary scenes I had read in novels actually true? In that moment, I was playing a part in a story called "The Harlequin and the Dying Nun" and all that remained was for me to find a guitar and serenade my beautiful Corinda (even this a name from a book), so that an old, nostalgic melody would be the last thing she heard before dying.

At times, all of reality conspires to turn itself into romance, a falsification of itself to the point of artificiality. This capacity for infinite possibilities is one of its special powers.

Just as I was about to leave the room, the sick girl appeared to be suffocating, and the doctor forced her jaws open to insert the tube from the oxygen tank, keeping her mouth open so that her teeth would not bite down and shatter the whole thing into pieces that could choke her. This scene had been omitted from the romance novels of my childhood. The room was filled with the pleasant smell of burning incense the patient had requested that afternoon.

When we found ourselves back in the corridor, the night air bit into us, cold and sharp. The lounge was empty, the lights were off, and the furniture in disarray, and through the large windows that opened onto the garden we could see snowflakes, slowly sifting through the blurred darkness of the night sky. Where had everyone gone?

Only the patients on stretchers had retired to their rooms. According to the cook, who was washing the dishes, the Englishmen, the motorcyclist and two nurses had gone to the nearby woods.

"They've all gone to the woods . . . it should be easy to find them . . . the motorcycle headlamp will be ablaze . . . make sure you don't get lost, though . . . just follow the path."

"So, shall we?" I asked the marquise. But she had already gone to the hall, put on her coat and was quietly opening the door. I followed on my crutches.

It was in fact a straight path through the forest but we couldn't see anything in the darkness apart from the faint glimmer of snow at its edges. As we entered the woods, just a few steps away from the sanatorium, the darkness was as thick as the pines themselves. Somewhere within its depths we could see a bright light, so we headed towards it.

It was warm and cosy in the clearing, the canopy of branches sheltering us from the falling snow as we walked on a soft, fragrant carpet of pine needles past benches placed there for resting, and the motorcycle headlamp filled this vegetal chamber with a blinding light in which the nurses' uniforms took on a dazzling sheen. Everyone was blind drunk, rolling around on the carpet of pine needles, singing lewd songs. They had changed into their normal clothes and the motorcyclist had taken off his turban. I was the only one still in costume, a harlequin gone astray in the night, lost in the woods, caught in the glare of a motorcycle light. I had no idea what I was doing there, what any of it meant, how we ended up stumbling around in that flood of light. The darkness surrounded us like thick wine, and we had curled inside our little nest of light while around us sleep and dreams dissolved in the blackness, dripping slowly through this dark wine into the skullcups of slumbering souls, intoxicating them with the heady liquor of terrible images and visions. And in the sanatorium lay "the beautiful nun" with her sliver of light and the vigil approaching its end, evaporating into the darkness. So many lives had expired and evaporated into this darkness, yet it remained thick and dense, bearing no trace of the lives that had trickled through it.

And there I was, in my bizarre harlequin clothes, submerged in the depths of night, where so many had drowned without a trace, and I couldn't understand it, however hard I tried, I couldn't understand anything.

And I was singing a melody and my mouth uttered the words everyone else was singing and I understood nothing.

Our song, too, drowned in the depths of the night without a trace.

It was late and there I was in my strange outfit, bathed in light.

Human lives evaporate into darkness, from darkness they come and into darkness they dissipate like the smoke of dreams rising from slumbering bodies, a darkness that engulfs the reality of days and all the objects within it, all of them absorbed and dissolved into this gloom. In the waters of oblivion only sounds float like timber, adrift on its waves, objects audible yet impalpable, a cry in the night, a thin wire stretched out before you yet impossible to grab, snoring and tiny husks of silence fall out of night into the darkness and fill the room, and you can't hold it in your hand, you can't grasp a fistful of snoring, a fistful of sound shells, and then toss them into the washbasin like you might peanut shells. Matter lurks in the darkness, performing tricks like a magician.

"Please pay close attention, there's nothing in my hands and nothing up my sleeve . . . I just need to light a match . . ."

And here is the wardrobe, my bedlinen, my hand.

There are different layers of darkness, like geological strata thickening through the ages. There is the porous, weightless darkness preceding sleep, absorbing our internal murmurs and the words floating through our bodies like a sponge slowly bloating with water; there is the cinema darkness, sliding on ropes of light that end in a dance of shadows on a flickering screen, in time with the music; and there is the empty darkness, dry and hard as coal, which is at the end of the corridor you go down when you've taken a deep gulp of chloroform.

After their operations, the patients would swap stories about the sensations and visions they had while lying anaesthetised on the operating table. When it was my turn, I had nothing to share because I hadn't felt or seen anything, no shadowy mountains, no echoing silence, my body had not floated over wide open plains. Perhaps I'd been enveloped in a sleep deeper than all the other patients, and I experienced none of the things they described.

Actually, this is what happened: It is a well-known fact that on the operating table patients struggle to get to sleep, their lungs rejecting the chloroform. But to the great astonishment of the doctor who placed the mask on my face, I began to deeply inhale the chloroform into my lungs until I was exhausted, as if I had been starved of air and was desperate to breathe in the anaesthetic. My violent attempt to absorb the contents of the cylinder prompted the doctor to remove the mask, probably fearing that I might faint or damage the equipment:

"Take it easy, please," she said, "breathe in more slowly or you could crack the valve. You are a remarkable patient, most of the others can't stomach the chloroform."

But I had my own reasons for this, hidden deep inside me. When I found out I was going to have an operation, I told myself: here is a wonderful opportunity to escape life in a simple, painless manner. This thought had been humming through my head for a long time and had transformed into an overwhelming desire. I had, in fact, already made a few feeble attempts to kill myself. I was a bit of a coward. I needed a simple, infallible, painless way out.

"When they give me the chloroform, I'll inhale it so deeply it will kill me," I told myself. "It's a straightforward, easy death, and no-one will know that I intended to end my life . . ."

I did slip inside a heavy darkness, dense and opaque, but it wasn't final. When I woke up, the room was askew, as if tilted at a right angle, and it took a few seconds to regain its balance, like in those films when the camera tilts and the whole scene glides through a valley only to return to the exact same place a moment later.

That darkness left me unsatisfied, and now I still crave — calmly, sometimes with an exasperated patience — the complete, irrefutable darkness of death.

Until that moment arrives, all that remains in my life are night and rain, the night for its dreams and benevolent darkness, the rain for its silence, for all the sadness, all the melancholy that rages through veils of water heaved by the wind and blasted onto windows, marbling the glass with liquid roots and trees.

Gazing out of my window, or better still, the window of a train compartment, I see the raindrops begin their abortive journey down the glass, crawling down windowpanes blurred by steam yet still transparent enough to reveal the ashen, damp hills racing away from me, the miraculous rise and fall of telegraph wires and the locomotive's thin, bluish wisps of smoke, drenched by the rain and ravaged by the wind.

On bright days I hide in a gloomy room and sleep all day with my head buried under the covers, searching for darkness, loathing the sun. Only rain can exfoliate my soul's joys, in the same way that succulents need moisture to thrive. I sit in a warm train compartment, racing past fields, staring out of a window speckled with steam and rain. A familiar journey, the most beautiful journey of all. Sometimes I fall asleep on the train and wake up in the middle of the night in a brightly lit compartment, and the train passes small stations winking with anaemic lights, their platforms polished black by rain, and sometimes I see a stationmaster in a waterproof coat and a red cap, saluting the train, saluting the rain.

The feeble light of the lamps on the platform briefly catches the branches and yellowing leaves of the autumnal trees before they slip away, and in that patch of light their withered crowns of shivering leaves appear even more forlorn, more crippled by the cold, the essence of autumn itself, while the acacia trees around the station hide in the darkness, drenched to the core. It is autumn and my journey will last for years, through eternal rain, while the stationmaster will carry on endlessly, tirelessly saluting.

My final destination will be the grand station of darkness.

In Berck, I would ride in my carriage for miles through the rain, and the water would pour down my face as if it had been a tiled surface about to be scrubbed clean, while the rest of my body, lying on the stretcher, was covered by a canopy the length of the whole carriage, made from a tough, impermeable cloth, always warm and dry underneath and smelling of rotten hay and rancid, greasy harnesses.

The town was surrounded by dunes, and I think that all towns have their silent, solitary places where their lunatics roam and Gypsies raise their tents. Yet the dunes around Berck have a sandy, thorny, hunchbacked solitude, pierced by grasses gleaming like sharp swords in the rain and fleshy plants with bluish thorns. When it rained, the dunes seemed to stretch into infinity, and from the top of the largest hill the great ashen expanse of grasses and weeds looked like a leprous scab, while the solitude felt as tender as hospital pain or cemetery silence, enveloping your whole being, as even the air always emptied to leave you alone and desolate in a landscape as ordinary, grimy and wet as a dishcloth left to mould. And the sky ceased to exist, transforming into condensed rain, a dense, brightening canopy, like a warm greenhouse where the moisture streams down the walls and steam fills the air.

Solitary, rain-soaked places can always be found at the edge of every town, and in my hometown I used to know one near the river, on a hill that was used as a trash dump. As I walked there, my feet would sink into the filthy, rotting, reeking pulp while I observed everything that sprang out of it: a chair leg, the hideous grin of an open tin can, a dead dog sleeping in the company of worms that squirmed in white waves when I turned the body over, some ribbons of an incredible shade of blue, a plant that had sprouted from the putrid matter, too fragile to survive the constant invasion of refuse, all of these remnants and traces of life, like a shipwreck sinking into this still, viscous sea, fuming in the rain, and the stench, ah! the stench . . .

I think this was where the little girls, my childhood friends, would find their beautiful beads. When I was a boy, we lived near a trinket shop that sold beads to peasants, tiny red beads like drops of blood, or glass beads like tears of mercury, or large blue ones like the bumps in a turkey's snood. The towns-people lined up their garbage bins by a wall in the communal courtyard, and my girlfriends would rummage through the trinket shop's bin in the mornings after the myopic shop-keeper had swept the floor and tossed out the dirt without noticing the beads mingled with it, and the girls rifled through the trash, pushing aside the chicken heads and feet the shopkeeper's wife had thrown away after preparing dinner, and the innards, like sleek, elastic necklaces, gleaming red with a blue iridescence, sometimes still held the shape of the undigested grain. It was amongst these intestinal necklaces that the girls sought the gleaming beads, delicately extracting them with long sticks.

But to find the most beautiful beads they had to venture to the dump at the edge of town. The mounds of garbage were large enough to spend a lifetime scouring for treasure. I would often see grubby folks with sacks on their backs, meticulously, slowly combing through the rubbish, and objects made of metal or rotten wood emerged out of the heaps of refuse. And they kept searching, unearthing all those everyday objects with which we are surrounded, objects that exist in ordinary houses, ordinary rooms where humans spend the hours of their days, expensive objects once bought in shops and carried home wrapped in fine tissue paper to be placed on shelves, dear, precious things that would bring a servant who had broken one an angry rebuke, or objects that have disappeared, or were damaged in some way, and rare books, rugs, porcelain figurines, all of them here, shattered, cracked, broken, lamentably ugly, mingled with putrid entrails and worms, trash fuming its filth in the rain.

All the things that surround human life belong to the worms and the trash heap, and our bodies will rot away like our entourage of fine objects. Everything is fated for corruption and putrefaction, and this is the lesson I learned wandering through the mounds of refuse, the lesson that filtered into the marrow of my bones, so that I no longer care for any object or even for my body. Everything must decay so that it can be absorbed into darkness, forever.

When I became more confident on my crutches, I found myself walking all the way to the village. Finally, I thought, I could meet some wonderful ladies and wheedle my way into a group of young party hounds. Although this did happen, to some extent, it was not in the way I'd envisaged. It was simple enough to insinuate myself into another sanatorium, I could easily find a reason for being there — my doctor worked in one such place further down the valley, a renowned clinic with many pensioners and a select clientele — and all I had to do was bring an X-ray with me and pretend that I wanted his opinion. To reach my destination as quickly as possible, I would take a shortcut through the woods next to my sanatorium. It was a narrow, steep path bordered by thickets. I remember these details because one day this route brought home to me the ferocious desperation with which I pursued these beautiful women.

It was a dry, sunny spring day and some of the patients from the valley were out walking in the woods. With the crutches tucked under my arms, dressed in my walking clothes and bareheaded, I climbed down the path towards my doctor's clinic. I was consumed by the thought that I would finally gain entry into those exotic rooms, but had no idea that my serene demeanour had been transformed by this thought until I came face to face with a mother and child in the middle of the path. I only became aware of my savage mien when I saw the terror in the mother's eyes as she dragged her child into the bushes to make way for me to pass, as if I were a car out of control or some rampaging beast. At that moment I realised that I was, in fact, out of control, racing downhill like a whirlwind, with giant strides, my cheeks ablaze, my hair tousled, like some feral drunk, my inner thoughts having intoxicated me and made me wild.

When I reached the clinic and opened the door, I noticed that its glass panels were vibrating, something I had put down on other occasions to its shaky construction, until I realised that today it was vibrating louder and more vigorously than usual because of my trembling hand. Once inside, I didn't inquire where I could find the doctor, preferring to wander down the corridors so that I could encounter the residents and strike up conversations with them. On this day I made an unexpected discovery that seemed to have been meant especially for me (a feeling I often had, that things had been designed particularly with me in mind . . .). It was a note, scrawled in thick blue pencil, pinned to one of the doors in the corridor:

DÉSIRONS VISITES.
VISITORS WELCOME.

This was the message, written in two languages, one of

which I didn't understand. Moreover, it requested exactly what I also wanted, to visit with someone. Before I knocked on the door, I imagined for a few moments that a beautiful creature, the girl of my dreams, was on the other side. But inside the room I found a shortsighted gentleman propped up on some pillows, a pair of glasses in especially thick frames perched on the tip of his nose, carefully studying an enormous book on his lap. It was a book on Danish law, and when we introduced ourselves, the man explained that he was a lawyer from Copenhagen and was almost cured of his illness, but incredibly bored, which explained the note he had put on his door. I was stuck with him now, and couldn't escape as quickly as I wanted because I had to listen to the details of his illness accompanied by his constant snorting, as he had undergone an operation on his sinuses and had tampons plugging both nostrils. I was ultimately rewarded for my patience because just as I was about to leave a young woman came in, a fellow Dane from another clinic who would visit her ailing compatriot to exchange magazines and newspapers. She was a young girl with golden hair, beautiful and shapely, wearing a long dress and a silk scarf around her hips — silk as golden as her hair — with the most extraordinary green eyes and delicate hands, who spoke French poorly, and it only took a few seconds for me to fall in love with her.

She told me where she was staying, a place not far away, and that she didn't have many friends. I asked if she would like to meet up from time to time, and she gladly accepted. I told her I would call on her the following day.

All night long I thought of her. I lay awake the entire night, feverish, a dreadful pain in my thigh, terrified by the thought that I might not be able to make it the following day.

It was snowing heavily the next morning and a thick white blanket already covered the path to the funicular. My head was pounding with fever, and everything around me seemed to be spinning, just like when I was a child and would spin in place until I nearly passed out, and the moment I stopped, I would fall to the ground and the world kept turning slowly like a record while I lay there at its centre. The ache in my thigh was steadily getting worse, growing stiffer and more inflamed until I couldn't move it normally, while my cheeks were on fire and I was sweating buckets. Despite all the pain, I tucked my crutches under my arms and started walking towards the funicular. It was snowing all around me, the landscape enveloped in a murky light, and I pressed on as snowflakes fell on my cheeks and, immediately melted by my fever, cooled them, sending a shiver through my body. The path climbed through the pine forest, and I was embarrassingly panting in my hurry to get there on time.

But when I finally reached the station, the car had already started and was halfway down the tunnel. I think it broke the stationmaster's heart to see the devastation on my face, so he whistled sharply and the car stopped inside the tunnel, in the dark. With considerable effort, guiding myself by the red lights at the rear of the car, I managed to reach it and get myself inside the compartment. At last I could sit down and rest my aching bones, and when the funicular started again I was so overcome by sweet lethargy that I easily drifted off to sleep, although making sure I remained alert enough not to miss my stop. But I was so drowsy I didn't realise I had gotten off at a station far below where I should have. It was too late to stop the funicular, so the only thing to do was to walk further down into the valley to find the path, then slowly make the climb back up to the clinic where the girl was staying.

I trust that these details will create an accurate impression of my mental state then and the cruel exhaustion that gripped me. It was this last leg of my journey, this pointless climb, that truly infuriated me. When I finally reached the clinic, I was told the girl was not in. I was livid as this was the last thing I expected, especially since I had telephoned her earlier that morning to ask if I could visit, and she said she was looking forward to seeing me. Feeling utterly dejected, I opened the door again to leave. Just then, the Danish girl appeared in front of me, holding a small package.

"Please forgive me, I just ran to the patisserie to get us something to nibble on with our tea . . ."

And she dragged me back inside, took off my scarf and coat, and started rubbing my hands to warm them up, incredibly effusive and friendly, so infectious that I forgot my exhaustion in a moment.

The room she took me to smelled of fine tea and lavender, and through the window overlooking the terrace we could see the snow-covered mountains, so decorative and theatrical that the whole room seemed like a stage set, especially with the gold silk cover on the bed and the bright blue walls, so that I felt like talking to her in the same way I used to speak to my child-hood friends when we were pretending to be in a play:

"Ah, dear baron, you remember in 1896, in Menton, I think, when we would take tea with the Marquise de Villemesson in her villa, eh, eh! Whatever became of her?"

Yet when the girl suggested I lie down and make myself comfortable, and I rested on the bed, I realised I wasn't feeling calm or confident enough to play at make-believe. All of the exhaustion and emotional torment had built up in my body and the fever was boiling beneath my skin. It was as if inside my arms and every fibre of muscle, in my head, in my chest, in my toes, a boiling liquid simmered so dense and thick it was beyond the realm of my experiences. In chemistry, there is a water with special properties that is heavier than regular water, so it is known as "heavy water." Well, my body had likewise become filled with "heavy blood." I felt like drifting off to sleep but couldn't even close my eyes despite the fatigue, because my torpor was equally mixed with an uncommon irri-tation and insatiable thirst to stir myself and to speak, to move my hands, my feet, maybe even to walk, and I'm sure I would have attempted to do so if my swollen, painful thigh hadn't kept me pinned to the bed. I then realised that I had pushed myself too far, that my efforts to reach this lovely, straw blonde, green-eyed girl and have tea and biscuits with her had been too great, too painful. I needed more and deserved so much more, I concluded.

When she sat next to me on the bed and asked if I was feel-ing all right, I took her hands and kissed them, then pulled her towards me. I think my actions were so rushed and febrile they left no room for hesitation. And to my extraordinary surprise, the girl didn't even protest when I started to undress her. It was something I deserved, I deserved everything. In a few moments, she was left wearing only her heavy silk slip, pleasant to the touch. And as she lay next to me, my fever found in that foreign body a receptacle for all the irritation and pain it had contained until then. With every caress, with every kiss on that delicate, cool, refreshing skin, I could feel all the animation inside me settling down until I reached a state of utmost tranquillity.

When I opened my eyes, it was late in the evening, the girl was still in the room, wearing a different dress, and I realised I had slept for several hours.

"Well, you should be ashamed of yourself . . . dozing off next to a naked girl." And she laughed quietly.

All my exhaustion had vanished, leaving me as slack as a rag doll, inert, sinking into that deep, dreamless sleep.

Over the following days I continued to visit her, and she would undress docilely, amiably, never tired and always full of surprises. Finally, I had found the beautiful woman I had dreamt of while I was lying immobilised in a plaster cast. During my walks around the sanatorium, I would connect everything that happened to me back to her. If the cleaning boy who scrubbed the floors didn't make way for me to pass, I would tell myself, with a certain pride:

"Eh, eh, if only you knew that I spend every afternoon with a beautiful naked woman . . ."

And if a voice inside me tried to argue:

"Maybe he wouldn't care . . . he's a member of a celibacy society."

Another voice would retort:

"Well, that's exactly why he would be interested."

In fact, everything I did somehow related back to her. I walked down the corridors with vain nonchalance because I knew a splendid, amazing girl would soon appear naked before me, and everything I touched, everything I experienced, melted in the wondrous light of this nudity.

Because she asked me to give her a name, I called her "Simpla," and later just "Si," but I never used her real name, which was Gerta.

When the spring rains came and melted the snow, the path to her clinic became so thick with mud that I showed up filthy and exhausted, and after taking off my shoes I threw myself onto the bed, sinking into delicious repose before I could even think of doing anything else.

"You know, I'm leaving in a few weeks," she told me one afternoon. "My doctor says I'm cured, so I will be returning to Copenhagen, my fiancé will come here to accompany me on the trip back."

"You're cured? You're engaged?" I peppered her with questions, uncertain what answer I wanted most.

"Yes, to both . . . But I noticed you never asked why I was here in Leysin and maybe you never would have if I hadn't told you I'm leaving . . . Cured, and engaged . . . Cured, after a difficult operation for an extremely serious case of peritonitis

. . . you saw the marks on my stomach, but you never asked me about them."

"Eh, when I see your naked stomach I'm thinking about other things . . ."

"Ah, very well!" she laughed quietly.

"As for my fiancé," she added, "I can show you a picture of him, if you like . . ."

She brought over a large, framed photograph of a blond young man with a dreamy expression who was staring wide-eyed at an extraordinary shaft of light coming from below.

"I keep this in my trunk, it makes things simpler . . ."

"You really are 'Simpla' . . . And when did you say he was coming?"

"In a few days, he will stay with me here for a month . . . and then, of course, we won't be able to meet like we do now . . . well, anyway, you understand . . . I'm engaged."

And she said this very firmly. It kind of made sense, I suppose.

But I allowed myself to imagine that this fiancé wouldn't be with her all the time, that he would go on outings and leave us alone occasionally.

During the first few days after her fiancé arrived, Si didn't phone me at all or write any notes, but one day she sent a message to inform me they would both be coming to take tea with me that very afternoon.

It was a beautiful sunny day and I thought we ought to stay out on the terrace for as long as we could, because it was more spacious. I had also invited another friend who needed to remain lying down, which he could not have done in my room. We were all in a good mood, and the fiancé, who was a keen chess player, suggested a game to the Englishman. I was now practically alone with Si, and on the pretext that I wanted to show her an engraving, I invited her to my room. As soon as I shut the door behind us I tried to kiss her. She pushed me away with a somewhat brutal, unmistakable firmness.

"What do you want?" she asked me, surprised. "You know I'm engaged and that my fiancé is right here . . . we can still be friends . . . but that's all . . ."

"Yes, but when you were apart, weren't you still engaged then?"

"Of course, but thousands of kilometres were between us and the power of an engagement is dissolved by such vast distances. Yes, there were letters, and every so often they brought me the distilled 'essence of engagement,' and on the days I received one of those letters I didn't allow you to see me . . . but once the letter was a day old, that essence evaporated, lost its power, just like a flower whose scent fades with time, until it loses its perfume altogether . . ."

I felt jealousy for the very first time in my life during this period, and even though my "girlfriend's" explanation was fairly clear and logical, it didn't satisfy me. I think my suffering was more intense than any of the physical torments I had experienced. Maybe this is the reason why I'm even recounting this story, because I think one of the most astonishing things in the world and in life is when a suffering such as this bestirs in the warm bundle of muscles, intestines and blood that add up to a human being, a suffering that is completely alien to them and produces no exterior physical alteration, nothing tangible or visible, spawned out of nothing, having invaded our dark inner self, churning terrible torments even though it doesn't comprise even a single atom of physical matter. It is astounding and insane. This insubstantial, bitter pain can turn life into tragedy, and then a moment later something equally intangible can distract us from this suffering. And like this, in this insubstantial, emotional realm, gripped by spasms of pain, understanding nothing, is how we live out our days. In this vacuum we create feelings that are merely segments of emptiness, existing only in our immaterial inner world, and delude ourselves that we live in the world, while in fact we are trapped in this void that absorbs everything, forever.

Everything we do, everything we think, all of it completely dissipates into the air, gone forever.

The air absorbs all of our actions and they disappear without a trace — I lift up my arm and the air swallows up the gesture and closes again, clear and indifferent, as if nothing had disturbed it.

Think of a magnificent ancient tree that for over a hundred years has stretched its branches skywards, hungrily embracing more and more air, more and more volume, growing taller and thicker. And look, when the trunk is severed at the root and the whole empire of rustling leaves collapses, the air holds no memory of its century-old strivings. All the effort of the sap surging from the roots right to the crown, the opacity of its thousands of leaves and the distinctiveness of each of its thousands of branches — none of this leaves any mark on the air, none at all.

When you walk down the street and glance behind you, there is nothing in the air to mark your passing.

When you fall silent after speaking, there is no trace in the air of the words you just uttered.

We are locked inside this terrible transparence, more impenetrable than any cell, we struggle inside it and all our actions melt away. Everything we have ever done, every moment we have lived, melts in the air, and the air restores its shape as if none of it ever happened. Our life is absorbed into all the world's clarity. And still, in this void buried inside our bodies there is something painful, an immaterial suffering detached from the physical world, thoughts and feelings bred out of nothing that torment our inner self, the very self that's also preparing to disappear and dissolve into the air.

It is one of the most astonishing things in the world to me, this jealousy that is so keenly felt but cannot be seen and leaves no physical trace. And the things we call love, or pain, all of it just fragments of nothingness, yet they all tear our inner worlds into bloody shreds.

But just like everything else, even my astonishment will dissolve in the air.

V

RATHER THAN AS A SUCCESSION OF EVENTS, IT MIGHT BE better to recount the story of my memories and thoughts as a succession of rooms, each with its own particular light, frequently gloomy and wistful, rooms suffused with the glow of rain, where I lay, eyes open, observing the life draining from my slack, inert body, while my ashen consciousness filled with the sensation of no longer existing.

Amongst the long series of sanatorium rooms I've inhabited over the years, perhaps the saddest and most dramatic was the one on the Black Sea coast where I had to stay for a few months after I returned from abroad. It was a huge sanatorium that operated like a factory. We were awoken by the ringing of a bell, and called to dinner and commanded to go to bed in the evenings by the same bell. All day long we would hear the buzz of other alarms around the operating theatre and watch hospital gurneys constantly going in and out as if it were a laboratory designed to transform human matter, to correct and improve it. In another large room other engineers — by which

I mean doctors — assisted by nurses dressed in white, were busy fitting plaster casts, while somewhere at the end of the corridor was a chamber with a large, rounded metal contraption full of screws and electrical leads into which bodies entered to be X-rayed exactly in the same way that objects would be put in a factory furnace. And all of this happened in silence, with languid movements and hushed whispers.

During the summer months, the patients were lined up on a terrace that faced the sun and the sea, bronzing their naked bodies. When I was a child, I spent a few wonderful years with my grandfather, who had a pottery factory at the edge of a provincial town, and he used to load his ceramics into enormous carts and take them to the various local markets. I liked to wander alone through the factory, and I got to know it pretty well. There was one particular spot where they would line up the ceramic pots to dry in the sun, and the first time I saw the tanned bodies on the terrace of the sanatorium, dark brown and earthen, I remembered the pots set out to dry in my grandfather's factory. They were exactly the same as that pottery, only broken in places and repaired with white plaster.

The patients stayed out on the terrace all day and in the evenings came back inside to dine and then retire to bed. Their dormitory was at the back of the terrace, you just had to open the doors to find yourself once again in the sun and the fresh air, on the strand, a few metres above the sea. It was like a long greenhouse, a kind of stable with a row of glass doors, and the light that came through them seemed more cold and hostile than it did outside. At the back was a long white wall where the patients were lined up in a row on their gurneys, so closely packed together there was barely any space between them and the doors. It was essentially a long, white, clinical corridor crammed with patients and filled with a deafening clamour. I think over three hundred gurneys must have been parked there. The few adult patients were separated from the rest by two thin screens into male and female sections.

On the first evening, after spending the day sitting in the shade on the seafront to take the air, I tried to go to sleep amongst the other patients in the greenhouse. Some of them had hoped to sleep outside, but a very windy night wouldn't allow it.

All the doors had been closed to keep us warm, then suddenly the white, tight space teemed with the noise of three hundred children all talking at the same time, whispering, breathing, coughing and singing. The singing was the worst of all. After dinner, they started bellowing in unison some annoying songs whose choruses were well known in the taverns, three hundred mouths screaming out the words in an indescribable racket, like a violent tempest of sounds. The onslaught of noise grew louder and more threatening until I feared the walls would crack and the ceiling collapse and the glass doors shatter into pieces.

I could have put up with this din if it weren't for other, quieter, more furtive noises hidden underneath it, sounds whose origins I struggled to distinguish. The curtain of noise was designed to conceal the bowel movements of three hundred children before bedtime. Within a few minutes, a gust of atrocious, nauseating stench began to circulate around the room, mingling with the tempest of noise. So that was the explanation! I suppose ears must be exceptionally resilient because I could endure the assault of the interminable singing, but I'm positive no nose could withstand the interminable flood of nauseous odours that relentlessly invaded the greenhouse with the same fury of the songs being belted out.

Honestly, I could have put up with anything apart from this, so I asked if I could sleep in the sanatorium's main building and then go out on the terrace for treatment during the day, and benevolently — there was so much benevolent understanding in the sanatorium — my wish was granted. But I did manage to make friends with the child patients pretty quickly, and there was always a gaggle of them around my bed reading me their poems or showing me their stamp albums, to which I contributed my own foreign stamps whenever I received letters from abroad.

It was a quiet sanatorium where I lived a tranquil life, but also where I experienced some horrific moments, periods of true despair and even great misery.

Everything that happened to me was veiled in an extraordinary, hallucinatory atmosphere.

On the upper floor, at the end of a corridor, there was a small room overlooking the sea. When I opened the window and looked out at the great expanse of the ocean, with the enormous building of the sanatorium behind me, I felt as if I were on a rocky promontory with the waves crashing around me, lashed by the wind — the wind howling around the room like a sinister choir — the room a headland or the bridge of a ship, with me at the helm, steering the sanatorium, a huge vessel, across the stormy waves into the night.

It was the only room I could afford, where I could be alone, and of course it was uninhabitable. Up until just a few days before I moved in it was used to store all the dirty laundry and the cleaners' equipment as well as some mousetraps — yes, these were particularly pertinent.

When I requested the room, I was taken for a lunatic and warned that it was tiny, freezing and infested with mice. There must have been a whole nest of mice because when I opened the door for the first time they started scurrying in all directions, squeaking, before disappearing into the wall through their little holes. It was almost winter; until then I had shared a room with another patient, but a craving for solitude impelled me to insist on having my own space, and eventually I was given this room. Besides, it would be easy enough to fill the mouse holes, furnish a small wardrobe and a desk, paint the walls, clean the windows and then wheel me in on my bed. No more than a day's work.

I insisted, I pleaded, and ultimately everything was done according to my wishes, and I remember the immense joy I felt on that first evening, tucked up in my bed, in my freshly painted room, alone, completely alone. The howling wind dancing around the building, the roaring sirens of the distant port, the crashing waves, all of it gave me the feeling of lying suspended above a storm, floating on the night, unshackled

The holes in the wall which had been filled now gaped open, round, hollow and black. "Beautiful," I said to myself, admiring the holes in the same way my doctor would admire my wounds, murmuring: "Beautiful fistula, red, round and hollow . . ."

I poked at the holes with a stick but heard nothing, no mouse ran out. The cement was terribly cold and I was shivering violently, and as I looked up from the floor the room seemed unfamiliar, as if I had truly embarked on a journey into a fantastical realm. And the holes, the black, round holes in front of me, stared at me with their eyes of darkness, as if they were watching me through hollow sockets. I gazed back at them in mute stupefaction. Here, in front of me, unmistakably, were two cavernous orbits, and it was as if I were inside an empty skull and gazing through its barren sockets at the world outside. Aha! This was it! I remembered everything. Why had it taken me so long?

One spring, in the ravaged snow far from town, on one of the thawing plains covered with garbage and animal carcasses smouldering in the sun, I discovered a dead horse on which the wolves had feasted through the winter and was now rotting in the balmy, humid spring air, teeming with the hum of flies and cockroaches shifting through its remains. Everything about it was filthy, putrid, the rancid, green flesh transformed into a viscous liquid draining out of the decomposing muscles, but the head, well, the head was splendid, like ivory, utterly, utterly white, because the insects had scavenged the flesh all the way to the bone, leaving behind a superb skull with its large yellow teeth exposed, an incredible work of art fit for display in a vitrine next to fine porcelain and expensive ivory objects. Its dark, empty eye sockets stared at the hallucinatory sun and the decaying plain. The skull was so clean and so beautiful it seemed like a drawing, and as a matter of fact its ligaments resembled fine, exquisite calligraphic marks etched on the bones with the utmost sophistication and skill.

And how had I not remembered this? Here were the same black holes watching me now, watching me from the other side. I was inside the skull, the horse's skull, in the splendid, barren emptiness of those sere bones. Was my room just an ordinary room? Were the cracks in the walls really just cracks? Everywhere I looked I recognised the skull, its osseous, ivory chamber, and the cracks in the walls were the ligaments holding its bones together. And that row of long, yellow objects grinning at me, were they books or teeth? They were teeth, they were, truly, the teeth of the horse, and I was inside its skull, inside its skull. Its rotting corpse stretched far behind me. The whole sanatorium lay there, entirely decomposed. With its exposed ribs, swarming with cockroaches and worms that gnawed on its corpse. And not only the cockroaches, but now the invading mice as well joyfully munched on the carrion, on the putrid sanatorium filled with purulence and decomposed flesh, forgotten in the tempest, below the cawing of the crows and the howling of the winds.

I lay on the cement floor, shivering from the cold, and didn't know what to do.

AFTERWORD

MAX BLECHER WAS BORN IN 1909 INTO AN AFFLUENT
Romanian Jewish family in the Moldavian provincial town of
Botoşani, but he grew up in Roman. At the age of 18 he left for
Paris, hoping to eventually embark on a medical career. In a
cruel twist of fate, he became a lifelong patient instead of a
doctor, receiving treatment in various tuberculosis sanatoria in
France, Switzerland and Romania, and ultimately losing all
hope for a cure. In 1934, when Blecher became resigned to the
fact that his illness was incurable, he returned to the peaceful
anonymity of Roman. Moving into a house with a garden,
where he was attended to by a live-in staff and received daily
visits from a doctor, he started the long, exhausting process of
writing his books. It was at once therapeutic and torturous.
With knees sightly raised and a small wooden table placed on
them, he wrote almost daily, determined to fulfill the almost
sacred mission of revealing his literature as an act of supreme
defiance of death.

Blecher wrote *The Illuminated Burrow* on his deathbed and

finished it a few days before May 31, 1938, when, at 28, he lost his battle with Pott's disease, or tuberculosis of the spine. His life story is just as strange and unsettling as his trilogy of novels, all written in the last four years of his life (*Adventures in Immediate Irreality* and *Scarred Hearts* are the other two). Together they comprise a vast narrative of physical suffering charting his odyssey through a medical inferno. In the guise of fiction, Blecher documents his unexpected diagnosis and desperate search for treatment, presenting a remarkable tale of suffering that could be situated in the larger paradigm where medicine and literature intersect, which is a longstanding tradition in the West. A pathography with distinct roots in Surrealism, Blecher's writing formed its own unique mythology that transcended Romanian modernism, namely, it was the mythology of a young writer who died prematurely at the end of a long journey in which he devoted unimaginable energy to turn his suffering into an authentic literary art.

Before the era of antibiotics and chemotherapy, bone tuberculosis was, with rare exceptions, a death sentence. Lesser known than the romanticized affliction of pulmonary tuberculosis, the bone variant is an evil cousin causing irreparable damage beyond the initial site of infection, the lungs. How Blecher became ill is uncertain. His sister, Dora Wachsler Blecher, claimed it all started with a football match at school when a fellow player accidentally hit him with a boot to the back. Yet a medical description of the disease would suggest that the pathogen actually begins in the lungs and then migrates to proximal bone structures in the body, particularly the ribs and vertebrae, causing their erosion and turning hard tissue into pus-filled caverns. *The Illuminated Burrow* details his extensive sanatoria experience in France, at Berck-sur-Mer, in Switzerland, at the alpine resort village of Leysin, and in his native Romania, at Techirghiol.

Back in Roman to spend the last years of his life writing, Blecher's letters to friends and fellow writers document his avid involvement in the literary life of his time. The Romanian cultural climate of the late 1930s was turbulent and virulently anti-Semitic. Avant-garde writers were a favorite target of the right-wing press, who relentlessly attacked them for a supposed lack of morality. Blecher himself, along with fellow writer Haimovici Bonciu, were subjected to such scurrilous attacks. What Ovidiu Papadima wrote in the extremist magazine *Sfarmă-Piatră* is just one example: "Bonciu and Blecher and their ilk are such geniuses the Jewish literary trade should work just as well as it does in all the other areas where we are systematically robbed."* The Surrealist writer Geo Bogza, Blecher's closest friend and confidant, a promoter of the Romanian avant-garde and revolutionary author in his own right, was tried and twice incarcerated for pornography, in 1933 and 1937. After Blecher's death, Romania's fascist fate was sealed by the dramatic ascension to power of the Iron Guard and General Ion Antonescu, one of Hitler's most fervent admirers.

---

*All translations from the letters and the press are mine; translations from *The Illuminated Burrow* are by Gabi Reigh.

After a few years in Roman, Blecher decided to rip up over 150 pages of his work in a suicidal crisis reminiscent of Kafka's own oeuvre-destroying impulses. According to Mihail Sebastian, whose *Journal* is one of the most comprehensive documents on interwar Romania, Blecher destroyed 80 pages of the new novel and 70 pages from a journal, while likewise threatening to end his life. Yet by Christmas that year he had read a few pages from *The Illuminated Burrow* to Sebastian and expressed his satisfaction with the result.

The Illuminated Burrow is, as the subtitle states, a "sanatorium journal," and although the novel is indeed a journal, it is not one in the usual sense as Blecher eschews linear chronology and the sequentiality of journal entries. Instead of entries with dates or places, there is the continuous flow of a hyperactive mind confessing its dreams and tales. Blecher's protagonist is an alter ego who, like the author in real life, is stuck horizontally on a gurney, moving only with assistance, dependent on caregivers, unable to take part in the most basic activities.

The novel documents the gradual loss of physical integrity, the fear and loneliness of everyday life in early 20th-century medical institutions that were treating a massively painful disease, the dull, relentless ache accompanying the decomposition and festering of bacteria-eaten bone. Trapped in a heavy, cumbersome cast, his chest, vertebrae and spinal column became fragile, unable to support him upright. Burning and itching, the skin underneath the cast turned pasty, smelled foul, dissolving into sweat and dirt. Exhaustingly painful punctions extracted pus from fistulae, relieving the accumulated pressure. Blecher's narrator doesn't shy away from the grisly details in an effort to make the pain real and perceptible, a shared experience between reader and fictionalized character.

More than a personal tragedy to Blecher, disease at times was an opportunity to explore his extravagant inner world, his nightmarish visions and the all-encompassing melancholy of his poetics. His novel is an exquisitely aestheticized confession of survival, created by the singular voice and consciousness of its protagonist. Alternating realism with vivid, delirious poetic images, Blecher portrays the world as an absurd funfair, a vast panorama of meaningless, incomprehensible gestures, a convulsive spectacle animated by weird characters caught up in awkward situations. Writing is the direct expression of life, its fundamental product: "Everything I write about was once upon a time real life," the narrator warns, as if to caution us about the authenticity of his story. It is a multilayered story, encompassing the politics of Jewish identity to the metaphors of the ailing body, all wrapped around a nucleus of tragedy and loss. When dreamlike and hallucinatory, the reality of each day becomes bearable.

Illness is an undeniable source of pain, but also an invisible bridge to a rediscovered intimacy with the secret life of the body: "I always discover the same tremulous darkness, the same intimate and familiar cavern, the same burrow, warm and illuminated, flickering with shadows, inside my body, the substance of my 'self' lying on the 'other side' of the skin." Blecher's fictional territory is irreality, the uncanny, yet

familiar counterpart of everyday life, a distinct continent out-
lining his work's imaginary geography. Alienated by disease,
the body becomes an integral part of this territory, a dark,
violently organic hiding place, like a cave harbouring waterfalls
of blood: "I feel my blood coursing through obscure channels,
in serpentine, living streams, digging its way through dark
flesh, connecting nerves to bones, its low, pulsating murmur
drowning in the body's night."

The darkness inside the body is a unifying element that con-
nects the individual to an endless journey, starting before birth
and ending in the Tenebrae of death: "Human lives evaporate
into darkness, from darkness they come and into darkness they
dissipate like the smoke of dreams rising from slumbering
bodies . . ." This perspective nourishes a grave existential
despair, voicing an essentially cynical view: "All the things that
surround human life belong to the worms and the trash heap,
and our bodies will rot away like our entourage of fine objects."

Erotic adventures, improbable projections of a feverish,
delirious imagination, are also contaminated by the spectres of
disease and physical decay: "And I dreamt of splendid chambers where beautiful patients with rouged cheeks and attired
in peignoirs barely concealing their nudity invited me to spend
the siesta hours in their company, and every afternoon [. . .] I
would meet and fall in love with fascinating naked countesses
adorned with pearl necklaces and magnificent bracelets . . ."

In his last letter, dated May 10, 1938, sent to Geo Bogza,
Blecher seemed hopeful and in good spirits, unaware of his
imminent demise. His appetite was good – "I think today I'll

eat chicken" — and he was looking forward to enjoying a beautiful spring day — "it's warm and sunny out, I might go out on the terrace." Referring to *The Illuminated Burrow*, he mentioned his intention "to try and finish it this month." The last chapter of the novel, focusing on his experience in Techirghiol, is significantly shorter than the Berck and Leysin sections, more of a sketch than a full narrative, with an ending that appears abrupt. There is no written record of Blecher's final days, but the eerie imagery of the novel's last pages: at the end of a strange adventure, the protagonist lies naked on the floor, shivering, unable to tell reality from nightmare, as he contemplates the skull of a dead horse by the side of a road. In this ultimate intimation of death, Blecher prefigured his own demise, as writing and dying have always been tightly intertwined in his life and art.

This translation into English of *The Illuminated Burrow* comes at a time when the significance of illness, suffering and dying bear unprecedented meaning. The global crisis precipitated by a pandemic has transformed values, discourses and rituals, with sickness and death omnipresent in everyday conversation. It has been a time of retreat to private spaces, a shift to introspection and reconnection with our bodies and inner worlds. Reading Blecher, a visionary European author who mapped the unreal, can be a therapeutic act.

Gabriela Glăvan
Timișoara, 2022

NOTE ON THE TEXT

This translation was based on the first full edition of *The Illuminated Burrow* edited by Saşa Pană and published in 1971 in Bucharest. The version that appears in Max Blecher's collected works, edited by Doris Mironescu and published as *Opere* (Bucharest: Academia Româna, 2017), was likewise consulted. Mironescu's placement of textual breaks somewhat differs from the earlier edition, and he has each section beginning on a new page, as if a separate chapter. We have decided to follow Pană's organization of the text with five chapters having section breaks within as this seemed the least disruptive to the flow of images and ideas, a particularly salient feature of Blecher's prose. Even so, at times some paragraph or section breaks within a chapter follow the Mironescu edition, that is, where Pană might not start a new section but Mironescu does, or they start in different places, we were guided by which of the two made the most sense to us. Some paragraphs are formed as well at the translator's discretion.

Self-portrait, 1934

BIOGRAPHICAL NOTES

MAX BLECHER was born in Botoşani, Romania, on September 8, 1909, into a middle-class Jewish family. His father owned a porcelain shop. He spent his childhood and adolescence in Roman, and upon graduating high school left for Paris to study medicine, but soon became ill and was diagnosed with spinal tuberculosis. After spending six years in various sanatoria, he returned to Roman where, confined to bed, he began to translate (Guillaume Apollinaire inter alios) and to write, contributing to *Le surréalisme au service de la révolution* and other journals as well as corresponding with some of the leading artists and intellectuals of the day, such as André Breton, André Gide, Martin Heidegger, Ilarie Voronca, Léon-Paul Fargue, and Mihail Sebastian. His only collection of poetry, *Transparent Body*, was published in 1934, followed by the "novels" *Adventures in Immediate Irreality* (1936) and *Scarred Hearts* (1937). Although his final work of prose, *The Illuminated Burrow*, was written in 1937-38, it was only published posthumously, first in an abridged edition in 1947, and then in full in

1971. Often described as "hallucinatory" and "nightmarish," Blecher's writing is a kindred spirit to Surrealism and a major contribution to the 20th-century European avant-garde. He died on May 31, 1938.

GABI REIGH was born in Romania and moved at the age of twelve to the UK, where she teaches English and translates. As part of her Interbellum Series, she has translated interwar novels, poetry, and drama by Lucian Blaga, Liviu Rebreanu, and three by Mihail Sebastian. She was awarded the Stephen Spender Prize in 2017.

GABRIELA GLĂVAN is Associate Professor of Comparative Literature at West University of Timişoara, Romania.

THE ILLUMINATED BURROW
A Sanatorium Journal

Max Blecher

Translated by Gabi Reigh from the
original Romanian *Vizuina luminată*,
first full publication edited by Saşa Pană
(Bucharest: Cartea Românească, 1971)

Afterword by Gabriela Glăvan

Frontispiece and illustration on p. 6 by Max Blecher
courtesy of Vinea Press, Bucharest

Cover image by Jindřich Heisler
reproduced by permission

Cover and design by Silk Mountain

Set in Garamond Premier Pro / Univers 67

FIRST EDITION, 2022

Twisted Spoon Press
P.O. Box 21 – Preslova 12
150 00 Prague 5
Czech Republic
www.twistedspoon.com

Printed and bound in the Czech Republic by Akcent

Trade distribution :

UK & Europe

CENTRAL BOOKS
www.centralbooks.com

US & Canada

SCB DISTRIBUTORS
www.scbdistributors.com

Leysin - Sanatorium Populaire